Galaxy Cat

By Barwell Hollings

First Edition Copyright, 2022

By Barwell Hollings

Introduction

Galaxy Cat is inspired by two stories that I published previously in a compilation titled **Twisted Fantasy Stories**. Galaxy Cat begins with the short story, **Space Cat** and then launches into an action-packed space opera.

Felicia, the space-traveling cat is back as is her human friend, Billy Wilson. Felicia is now the captain of a starship, the Starkitty1. Her mission is to seek out and explore inhabited planets and moons in our galaxy. You will love the fun-loving collection of aliens that make up Felicia's crew.

With the help of space portal technology, Felicia and her crew jump from planet to planet and star system to star system in search of adventure. The action never stops. Nor does the endless variety of aliens that they encounter. Some aliens are nice, others, not so much. All are unique, fascinating and entertaining.

I hope that you enjoy Galaxy Cat.

Table Of Contents

First Contact

I will never forget the first time that I met Felicia. I was sitting on my backyard porch in Portola Valley, California. I live in a five-bedroom home on an acre and a half lot in this upper-class community. Portola Valley is a community where many wealthy Silicon Valley executives and venture capitalists have their homes. It is also the home for many of the areas

"horsey people". In addition to their Ferrari, Lamborghini and McLaren supercars, many of these folks also ride horses. There are stables and riding trails that thread through the local parks and open spaces. At the time that I met Felicia, I was a rather shy sophomore attending Menlo-Atherton High School.

Anyway, it's a pleasant summer evening, so I decided to step outside and sit on the porch swing. We have a large backyard with a stand of cedar trees at the far end. I am slowly swinging while looking up at the stars. The sky is clear, and the stars look

particularly bright this evening. I'm about to get up off the swing when I notice a streak of light shooting down from the sky. The streak seems to end behind the stand of large cedar trees. There is no noise from an impact. I am thinking, *what the hell is that?* I decide to walk over and see if a meteorite or other object may have landed in my back yard. I'm almost at the cedar grove when I can hear a low humming sound. As I round the outermost tree, I see a strange metallic cylinder sticking up from the ground. The cylinder is about six feet tall and appears to have some windows on its sides. There is strange marking on the cylinder that do not resemble anything that I have ever seen before. A door on the side of the cylinder opens and a

ramp is lowered. I'm not sure what I am looking at. Do I stay or do I back away? I had watched the movie, **War Of The Worlds** last week and there was a scene just like this where a creepy alien walks out of a space ship. I decide to stay and watch what happens next. I can see a furry paw emerge followed by another. Next, a furry head sticks out and looks around.

I'm standing there speechless. This furry creature walks down the ramp on all four legs. The creature resembles a large tabby cat. It turns towards me and gives me a wink of its eye. By now I'm thinking that

I'm going nuts. A tabby cat just stepped out of an alien spaceship and winked at me. Then a very strange thing happens. There is a voice inside my head that

says, "Greetings Earthling!" I'm thinking that I'm really losing my mind. *Did I just hear the cat greet me?* The cat stands up on its hind legs, pushes something like a keypad on the side of the cylinder and the ramp closes.

The creature turns to me again and projects its voice into my head once more. "My name is Felicia. I'm a space traveler from the star system you call Alpha Centauri. I have been traveling for five years at just under the speed of light. But now I have arrived on your planet. I'm very pleased that I can breathe your atmosphere. Oh, how rude of me. I forgot to ask, what is your name?"

I'm still speechless. I'm also at a loss as to how to communicate with this furry space alien. I decide to speak. "My name is Billy." The creature responds with thoughts projected inside my head, "I'm pleased to meet you Billy, may I also ask where on your planet we are right now? What do you call this location?"

I respond, "We are in the town of Portola Valley, California. California is in a country we call the United States." Then I pause and ask, "What are you doing here? Why does an alien spaceship land in my backyard?"

Felicia answers, "Oh, I see. This is probably a bit much for you to absorb all at once. Meeting aliens is probably not a common experience on your planet. My home planet is called Meowmax. We have been aware of your planet for thousands of years. In fact, our first explorers visited here more than three thousands of your years ago. They landed in a place that you call Egypt. They stayed for several years but then returned to Meowmax. We have visited a few times since then. Some of our space explorers were known to your ancient Greek, Norse and Chinese cultures." Felicia pauses then she begins again, "I suppose you want to know why we are here? And why we keep returning? Well, we are curious to see how things have developed on your planet. After all, Earth is the closest planet to Meowmax that supports intelligent life forms. I guess you could call us nosey neighbors." Felicia puts on an adorable kitty expression. I begin to relax a bit. It's hard to be afraid of this friendly furry alien.

I learned about ancient civilizations in my history classes. I also did research online for a paper that I wrote last year about gods that the ancients worshipped. Cat worship has come up in many ancient civilizations. Now I know why. These alien cats kept popping up every few hundred years. Perhaps they exerted some influence on Earth's ancient civilizations.

I ask Felicia what prompted this particular visit? She responds, "We have a radio sensing probe located in one of the outer rings of Jupiter. This sensor was

7

placed there, thousands of years ago to monitor radio transmissions from the Earth in the event that advanced technology is developed. For thousands of years nothing extraordinary was detected. In the last one hundred years your planet has begun to flood local space with all sorts of radio wave transmissions. Our sensor is sensitive enough to differentiate between transmissions from natural sources and those made by technologically advanced civilizations. When such a transmission is detected, the sensor deciphers it using a complex algorithm. Then it relays the relevant content to Meowmax. Our scientists were excited by the transmissions and decided to send me to investigate what is going on here."

I ask, "Why did you land in Portola Valley?" Felicia responds, "Why not? I'm kidding. Actually, if I landed into the center of a high population area, my ship's landing would more easily be detected. If I landed in the middle of nowhere, I would be too far from the technology that I want to observe. Portola Valley is neither the boonies nor the city. And as a bonus, I found you. It's perfect!" Again, Felicia turns on the charm with her big cat eyes.

I'm still feeling a little anxious, so I ask, "So what am I supposed to do? I'm just an average high school student. I'm not a scientist or politician or anything else of importance for that matter." Felicia responds, "You are a typical human growing up in a technological society. I can learn a lot from you. But I do have one question. Do you have a dog or a cat nearby? Dogs tend to get upset at my presence. They start barking uncontrollably. Your Earth cats tend to get territorial when strange cats are around them. There is a lot of hissing, youling and spitting. This has been a problem in the past for previous visitors from my planet. Sure, I can make myself invisible, but that only confuses them because they can still pick up my scent."

I respond, "I have a pet hamster and a parrot. I keep both in the house, in cages. This is a rather rural place so there are occasionally mountain lions, bobcats and coyotes lurking about. In fact, last week there was a mountain lion sighting just a few blocks away. It caused a bit of a panic among the neighbors."

Felicia responds, "Thanks for the warning. I will have to dial up my zapper." I ask, "What's a zapper?" She responds, "It's a small defensive device that I keep hidden in my fur. If I am cornered by some predatory creature, I activate it and then zap!" I say, "That sounds lethal." Felicia says, "Oh, it really does not harm them. It is a brief period of discomfort that motivates the predator to leave me alone. If they persist, I set it to a higher setting. That always works."

Felicia asks me, "Tell, me about yourself? What is your function here on Earth?" I think for a moment, then respond, "Well I'm a high school student, so I guess that my function is to obtain knowledge that I can use later in life." Felicia responds, "Oh, that's excellent. Perhaps you can share with me the tools you use for your learning experience. I was hoping to study the process by which young humans are introduced into a technologically advanced society."

I reach into my pocket and pull out my cell phone. I show it to Felicia. She looks at it and then asks, "Does it respond to both touch and voice commands? What about telepathy? All I can do for a voice is to jabber in my native cat language. But that will sound like a meow to you." She makes a series of meow sounds. Then she says, "See what I mean? I don't think your device can interpret what I am saying." She pauses and then says, "I will have to use the pads on my paws to make a manual query." Felicia raises her right paw. She extends each pad almost like a finger. She extends one and then the one next to it and so on. She says, "I bet Earth cats can't do that! We use the front four pads for typing on our computational devices. Also, when we extend the pads on our paws, we can hold onto objects and manipulate tools. That is how we developed technology. Someday your Earth cats may evolve sufficiently to do the same. It may take a hundred thousand of your Earth years for that to happen. They are quite intelligent even if they have not fully developed telepathy. They do have great body language though."

I ask, Felicia, "How long do you plan to stick around my yard. I ask because you have this spaceship that will certainly be noticed when the gardeners come to mow the grass tomorrow morning. She responds, "Not to worry, I will just make it look like a common object." In an instant, the spaceship fades away and a rock materializes. She says, "To anyone walking about, the spaceship will appear to be a rock. It will even feel like a rock if they happen to encounter it."

I respond, "That's a clever trick, but what about you? I'm sure that someone in my family will notice a large stray tabby cat hanging around." Felicia responds, "That's where I turn on the charm. You can tell them that I just started hanging around. I don't have a collar so there is no way to identify if I belong to someone else. Just pet me and start feeding me. I will look into their eyes with my cute kitty expression. It works every time. At least that's what the training manual says about how to charm Earth humans. It also does not hurt that I place a suggestion in their minds that it's ok to feed me until my owner shows up."

At this point, I'm really blown away by Felicia. She seems to have her stuff together. It's almost like I'm in a dream that does not end. I say, "Ok, you can stay here as long as you do not cause any problems." Felicia responds by saying, "Thank you Billy. But I have one more request. Please don't tell anyone about the alien kitty stuff. They will think that you are nuts." I reply, "Not to worry. It's to be our secret. Anyway, it's getting late, and I need to get to sleep. I have an early class tomorrow."

Felicia asks, "When will I see you again?" I reply that I get home from school around 3:00 but I need to start my homework and eat dinner. I'll be out on the porch around 6:00." Felicia responds, "I'll see you then.

Meanwhile, I will go back in my ship and see if I can break into the local wireless communication system."

I leave thinking that any minute I'm going to wake up from this dream. Yes, that must be it. I dreamed the whole thing up! So, I go upstairs, wash up and get ready for bed. I think to myself that when I wake up, the dream will be over. Tomorrow when I sit out on the porch, nothing will happen. In moments, I'm sound asleep.

I get up at 6:30 in the morning. I wash up, dress, gather my books and head off to school on my bike. I'm thinking that I really had a crazy dream last night. Classes go well. At noon, I have lunch with some friends. Somehow, we get on to the subject of dreams and nightmares. I'm tempted to tell my friends about the crazy dream that I had last night, but for some reason I decide not to. Felicia's words stick with me. *It's our secret.*

I get home about the usual time. I go to my room and work on some math homework and then go down to dinner with my family. My sister Emily is going on about how her best friend just broke up with her boyfriend. It's very boring stuff, but I listen anyway. My mom asks Emily and I to clear the table. We get it done fast and load the dishwasher. It's about 6:00 now and I'm in my room watching a YouTube video on my computer when I get the urge to go out on the porch. So, I carry my computer downstairs and sit down on the porch swing. I'm surfing around looking at videos when I feel something rubbing my leg. I look down and I'm staring into the furry face of a rather large tabby cat. The cat winks at me and I think, *oh, my god! It's not a dream! Felicia is real!*

The voice speaks to me inside my head. "Good evening Billy. Beautiful night isn't it! And, oh yes, I am real." Felicia jumps up into my lap and looks at the screen on my computer. She says, "That's real good screen quality that you have on this device. You humans have developed some good flat panel technology." She pauses and asks, "Do a search for Alpha Centauri. I want to see how fast the search results come up."

I do as Felicia requests and in a few seconds the list of results is displayed. Felicia then points to the fourth result on the list and asks, "Click on that one!" I do so and the icon spins for a few seconds before the results come up. Felicia comments, "Not bad throughput speed. I'm impressed. Can I give it a try?" By now, I'm completely dumbfounded. I'm thinking, *is this really happening? Or am I going nuts?* Felicia says, "Look at what this article is saying. The author is saying that the first planet orbiting Proxima Centauri cannot sustain life. Wrong! I'm from that planet and I can tell you that the author of this article does not know what he's talking about!"

I ask, "Are you really from the first planet orbiting Proxima Centauri?" Felicia responds, "I certainly am!" Just then my sister Emily walks out onto the porch and sees Felicia in my lap. She asks, "Billy, where did that cat come from?" Felicia turns to her and gives her the cute kitty look. Emily comments, "Oh, she is so cute." Emily reaches over and pets Felicia. Felicia starts purring. I tell Emily that the cat just walked up to me and sat in my lap. Emily says, "I'm going to go inside and get her some milk. She comes back with a small bowl of milk and puts it down on the floor. Felicia jumps down from my lap and starts lapping up the milk. Emily says, "Good kitty! Enjoy your milk!" Felicia sends me a thought. "See, a little charm works every time." She finishes the milk and says to me, "Not bad."

Then she jumps back into my lap. Emily goes back into the house with the empty dish.

Felicia says, "Can I take over surfing?" I reply, "I guess so." The next thing that I know, Felicia's paws are flying across the keypad. She finds an ad for our internet service provider. Felicia stops at the specifications page and looks it over. She says, "I'm impressed at how fast the wireless technology has progressed here. Ok, let's take a look at the news feed."

She finds the world news tab and clicks on it. There are stories about wars, protests, homelessness and crime. She comments that humans seem to not take very good care of each other. On Meowmax, there is not such a big gap between the rich and poor. Everyone seems to find a niche in cat society where they can be productive.

Felicia expresses an interest in visiting my school. She asks if I could take her there in the morning. I am a bit concerned with this request. I explain that I cannot take a cat into the classrooms. And what if you get lost and cannot find your way home? Felicia answers, "Not to worry, I can do my transformation trick whenever it's necessary to hide. I also have a small locating device in an implant under my skin. It can project a holographic map out of my right eye. It has built in directions and warnings. It's quite useful when I am exploring on foot."

I'm beginning to realize that Felicia is an experienced traveler who has all the bases covered.

My bike has side satchels attached to it. I use them to carry books and other things to and from school. I will use one of the satchels to carry Felicia with me to school.

It's the next morning. I just finished my breakfast and am ready to ride to school. Felicia comes running over and climbs into my side satchel. It's just big enough for her to pop her head out and watch while I pedal to school. She tries not to be too conspicuous. She comments that riding on the bike is fun. On Meowmax, they have a similar device that is driven by a system not unlike an elliptical bike. Of course, these are much smaller than human bikes and therefore not used for long rides. For longer rides, the cats use a scooter type device. She also comments about cars on the road." The cars are so big, and they hold so few humans. They are very inefficient and are dangerous too. Cars rely too much on human judgment and reflexes. They need more automation to be safe." I respond that we are working on self-driving cars with collision avoidance.

We have arrived at the high school bike racks. I tell Felicia that I will be heading home today at 2:30 and to meet me here at the bike racks. Next, I ask Felicia what she plans to do now that she is on campus? She replies, "Oh don't worry about me. I know how to get around and stay out of trouble. See you at 2:30. I must take a nature break right now." Having said that, Felicia jumps out of the bike satchel and takes off towards the bushes near the football field.

My first class on the day is biology with Mr. Smithfield. He is standing up at the blackboard drawing DNA strings and explaining the function of various nucleotides that are part of a DNA strand. I'm starting to get bored and turn my head towards the window. There, I see Felicia staring into the class. I can't talk to her, but I can hear her thoughts. She is commenting on how similar the DNA structure on the blackboard is to that of her species. I'm hearing a running commentary from Felicia about the lecture that Mr. Smithfield is giving. This is disrupting my concentration on the lecture, so I put out a thought telling Felicia to please be quiet. She replies, "Sorry."

For the rest of the class Felicia quietly absorbs the lecture.

Just before class ends, Felicia disappears from the window. I exit the classroom and walk to my second class. Second period is my geometry class. The lecture is on the Pythagorean theorem. Again, this is dry stuff, so I begin to daydream. I turn to the window and sure enough, there is Felicia again. She is watching the instructor write on the blackboard. This time Felicia is quiet and does not disturb my thoughts.

Class is over so I go to my locker and find my lunch. I take it over to a bench and sit down. In minutes, Felicia jumps up onto the bench and sits beside me. She asks, "Billy, what do you have in the bag?" I open the bag and say, "Peanut butter and jelly sandwich and an apple." She responds, "Blah! Not anything you would catch me eating." I pull out a small pack of cat treats and ask her. "Want to try these?" Felicia responds by taking a bite of one of the treats. She responds, "Not bad." So, I give her some more to munch on.

Felicia asks me if I have any female human friends. I respond, "Well, I'm not dating anyone right now."

The truth is that I'm too shy to ask anyone out. Felicia says, "I noticed you looking at that female human over there during class. I think you like her." I say, "Oh, her name is Lucy. She's not interested in me. She always hangs out with the athletes." Lucy is standing about twenty feet away talking to a group of people. Felicia responds, "Watch this."

Felicia looks in the direction of Lucy. Then she curls up in my lap. At once, Lucy looks our way. She stops talking to her friend and walks over to us. As she approaches, Felicia looks up at her with her adorable cat expression. Lucy says, "Hi Billy, I see you have a furry friend with you. Can I pet your cat?" I am a bit flustered but manage to respond, "Sure Lucy." Up until now, Lucy has never given me the time of day. Lucy sits down next to me and begins petting Felicia who is purring. Felicia rubs her head against Lucy's hand while she pets her. I'm nervous having Lucy so close to me. Felicia sends me a thought. "Relax Billy, I think that this female likes you. Lucy smiles at me and says, "Your cat is very nice. You know, I'm a cat person. What is your cat's name?" I respond. "Her name is

Felicia. She's not really my cat. She kind of adopted me and follows me around."

Lucy looks at Felicia and says, "Nice to meet you, Felicia." Then she looks at me and says, "See, we both have something in common. We both love cats. You should come over sometime and see my cats. Their names are Sydney, Louie and Sprite. Here's my phone number and address. Stop by if you get the chance." Then she gets up and says, "Bye Felicia, Bye Billy."

I'm almost speechless. Felicia says, "See, this female likes you, all you needed was some help from your feline match maker, me!" The bell rings for the next class, French. I remind Felicia to meet me at 2:30. Then I set off for class.

At 2:30 I walk over to my bicycle and unlock it from the rack. I peer into the satchel and see Felicia curled up and snoozing away. She awakens and says, "Hi Billy. It's been very informative following you around today. I learned a lot about how humans are educated."

I begin cycling back home. It's mostly uphill to get to my house. As soon as I get to the driveway, Felicia jumps out of the satchel. She tells me that she needs to go to her ship and record her observations for the day. She is expected to log daily entries describing her activities and findings. She tells me that I will be featured prominently in her report. Then she asks,

"Will I see you again at 6:00?" I respond, "See you then."

Felicia remained in my back yard for the next few days. Then one evening she tells me that she will be heading off to the next leg of her journey here on Earth. She even gives me an email address where I can converse with her as she travels. I think this is very strange but make it a point to stay in touch, nonetheless. *How does a cat get an email address?*

A few days later, I get an email from Felicia saying that she is in Greece. She is hanging out on the island of Santorini. Santorini is known as a place where there is a very high population of cats. She attaches a photo of herself posing in front of a beautiful view of the town with its white walled buildings and blue roofs. I do not ask how she managed to get this selfie. I have learned that Felicia is a very resourceful creature.

The next email comes from Egypt. She is posing in front of the Sphinx. Another photo is from the great pyramid at Giza. The next week, she sends me an email from Aoshima, the famous Japanese cat island.

The emails continue for the next two weeks. Each time, Felicia is in another place. Then one day I'm sitting on my porch thinking about Felicia and our strange interspecies friendship when I feel something rubbing against my leg. I look down and it's her.

Felicia jumps up onto my lap and looks me straight in the eyes. She tells me that her time on Earth has come to an end and it's time for her to move on to explore some of the other planets in the solar system. I'm a bit choked up. I say, "Felicia, I'm going to miss you. You have become a big part of my life since the day you landed in my backyard. I hope someday to visit some of the places that you have visited. Have a safe journey." I pick her up and give her a hug. Felicia says, "Billy, I'm going to miss you too."

Then she tells me that she will stay in touch with me while she is in our solar system. I wonder how she can do that, but remember that she is Felicia, the space-traveling cat. She could do anything.

Felicia jumps off my lap and walks across the yard and behind the stand of trees. In moments, I see a streak heading up into the star filled sky. It quickly disappears. I think that is probably the last that I will hear from Felicia. A few days later I get an email with a video attached. It begins with someone in a space suit jumping around what looks like a moonscape. There is an American flag standing there in desolate surroundings. The person in the spacesuit is doing summersaults and long leaps. It reminds me of the videos of the astronauts that visited the moon decades ago. Then the person in the spacesuit bounds over to the camera lens. I see a face inside the visor of the space helmet. It's Felicia. She must be on the moon.

I'm thinking, *how can she do that?*

A few weeks later, I get an email with a similar video attachment. She is holding up a plaque with the word **Mars** written on it. This steady string of emails continues over the next few months. There are closeup photos of asteroids, planets and moons. She even sends a video of a streaking comet.

As she travels further and further from Earth the time duration between the emails becomes longer due to the distances that the signals must travel. Her final email tells me that she hopes to run into me again someday out here in space. Until then, stay safe and enjoy life's adventures! *"Billy, you can reach for the stars."*

So now you know why I studied so hard in college and eventually received a doctorate in astrophysics.

Then I applied to NASA to join the astronaut program and was accepted. When applications were solicited for the Mars mission, I was the first application submitted. I was happy when I was selected as one of the candidates for the first manned mission to Mars. I realized that visiting Proxima Centauri was an unrealistic goal, but I wanted to be like my friend Felicia. She visited Mars so I wanted to go there too.

The training for the Mars mission was rigorous but I was up to the challenge. I probably had an advantage over the other candidates because I had a furry feline mentor flying around out in space. My happiest day was when I was selected for the mission. That night I looked out at the stars and thought of Felicia and the journey that my life has taken since I met her. She no doubt is traveling between the stars on her way back home to Meowmax.

The trip to Mars took eight long months. We were traveling at almost 25,000 mph. During the trip we had to keep in peak condition to overcome the effects of zero gravity in space. We had a rendezvous with a refueling ship. One of the things about space travel is that there is a lot of dead time when nothing is happening. I recall Felicia telling me that she was put in stasis during the long trip from the Proxima Centauri system to our solar system. We do not have that technology. Her ship also had propulsion technology allowing it to travel many times the speed of our ship. A trip to Mars could be done in days rather than months.

At last, we arrived and set into high orbit around Mars. The surface of the planet was reddish in color. From space, you could tell that there was not much atmosphere. The sun appeared much smaller from Mars than it does from Earth.

I, and my fellow astronaut, Larry Conway, are sent down to the surface in the two-person lander. The third crewmember, Captain Jennifer Swartz, remains on the ship, which continues to orbit the planet. Larry is designated as the first person to exit the Mars lander and take a walk around the surface of the planet. I watch as Larry dons his space suit and exits the lander. He climbs down the steps. Our camera captures Larry's first footstep onto the surface of Mars. I will have to wait until tomorrow morning before I get my turn.

It will take about five minutes for the video signal to reach Mission Control and the rest of planet Earth. I'm sure that back there, everyone is celebrating much like they did back in 1969 when Neil Armstrong stepped on the Moon.

Larry is walking around, then jumping long distances in the low gravity of Mars. He looks like he is having fun. Then a curious thing happens. A small object comes into view. It's flying about four feet above the Martian surface and approaching at a rapid speed. As it gets closer to Larry it begins to slow down.

The object looks like a smooth cylinder with no obvious source of propulsion. Larry says, "What the hell!" The object stops in front of Larry. The nose of the cylinder opens, and a thin mechanical arm extends outward with a rectangular flat object held in its gripper. The arm places the flat object at Larry's feet. The arm retracts back into the cylinder, which turns around and zooms off towards the Mars horizon. As soon as the object is out of sight, Larry says to me, "Billy, did you see what just happened? Am I going nuts out here?" I reply, "Larry, I saw exactly what you saw. I have video of the whole thing." I have no idea what that was, but I can tell you that it did not come with us. Then I ask, "Larry, reach down and take a look at the rectangular objcct."

Larry picks it up and says, "You're not going to believe this but there is writing on the object and it's in English. This is some kind of greeting card." I ask Larry to read what it says. Instead of reading it he turns to me and shows me the writing. I set the camera to zoom in on the card. I'm in shock. Larry asks me "Billy, who is Felicia?"

The card is in plain view now. It reads as follows,

Billy, welcome to Mars. You made it!
Your furry space traveling friend,
Felicia.

Eighteen Months Later

I'm sitting on a bench at Shoreline Park in Mountain View, California. The Mars landing seems so long ago. After we returned to Earth, there was an investigation into the greeting card that Felicia had left for me on Mars. Investigators from numerous government agencies were interviewing Larry and me about the card and the strange metal object that delivered it. Of course, Larry had no idea about who Felicia is. When I finally told the investigators my story, they thought that I was nuts. So, I asked them to put me through a polygraph test. They did so several times and my story held up. That did not deter them from disbelief about my story.

A rumor was spreading that a few months before the Mars mission, a probe was sent to Mars by a private space exploration company to provide the astronauts with a greeting. NASA decided not to throw any water on that rumor. The documentaries that followed the Mars landing played down the incident or did not mention it at all. All that was shown was Larry taking his first steps on Mars and later doing some exploring of the surface.

After the investigations were closed, I was quietly shown the back door. I received a severance check and sent on my way. It has been difficult for me to find a full-time job ever since. A kind of cloud has been hanging over me. I managed to get a temporary job for a few months at a laser company, but that ended three weeks ago. So, I'm sitting here enjoying the California sunshine and contemplating my next career move. I'm not married and have no children. I'm not even dating anybody. At this point in my life, nothing is holding me down. I'm thinking that I should take some time to do some travelling. I had put my live on hold for many years while training for the Mars mission. It's time to take a break.

Suddeny, I notice that I am not alone on the bench. I look down and see a large tabby cat looking up at me with a cute expression. There is something familiar about this cat. And then it hits me. I ask the cat, "Felicia, Is that you?" The cat responds with a telepathic voice inside my head, "The one and only!" I ask, "What are you doing here? I thought you were done with your exploration of our solar system and were going back to your home planet of Meowmax."

Felicia responds, "That was the plan. I did return to Meowmax just in time to learn that our scientists had made a huge technological breakthrough. They had developed a faster than light technology. I reply, "I thought that it was impossible for any propulsion technology to move an object faster than the speed of light." Felicia responds, "It has nothing to do with propulsion. Simply stated, our scientists invented a machine that opens a portal in space. The portal is a door that connects one location in space with another. Pass through it and you find yourself instantly at your destination. Of course, they also needed learn how to calibrate the machine so that you arrive exactly at the destination that you desired. The scientists also improved ship cloaking and teleportation systems. A lot had happened in the ten years that I was away from Meowmax. The leader cats at the space agency wanted an experienced space traveler to try out the new toys. I returned just in time to volunteer."

I say, "Wow, your scientists must have been collaborating with Mr. Spock and the Vulcans?" Felicia responds, "Nice Star Trek reference." Then she says, "Numerous prototypes were built and tested before they build the ship that I used to travel here. My ship is called the Starkitty1."

I say, "Felicia, it is good to see you again, but I do have a bone to pick with you. You got me in a lot of trouble with the greeting card stunt on Mars. It turned out that my fellow astronaut, Larry, was the first to step onto the surface of Mars. I was in the lander at the time. Larry picked up the note and then displayed it to the world on live video feed. The folks at mission control do not have a sense of humor. They were really upset and demanded answers." I pause to collect my thoughts and then say, "I had to tell them the truth about meeting you. They thought that I was nuts even though I passed all the lie detector tests they ran me through. I was quietly drummed out of the space program. That is why you find me sitting on this bench at two o'clock in the afternoon on a Tuesday. I'm having trouble finding any kind of meaningful work."

Felicia responds, "Gee Billy, I'm very sorry about that. I thought I was welcoming you. It took a lot of programming and planning to set the whole thing up remotely while I was billions of miles away traveling back to Meowmax."

So, I say, "Felicia, don't worry about it. I did get to walk on Mars the next day before we took off to return to Earth. But I was hoping to go on more missions in the future. I guess that's out of the question since I was kicked out of the program."

Felicia is quiet for a moment but then says, "Well Billy, you may yet get to go back into space, and sooner than you may think." I respond, "How's that going to happen?" She answers, "You can come with me!" I say, "What?" Felicia explains, "My ship is in orbit and it's quite large. With portal technology, there is no longer a need to have the lowest mass on our ships. My ship has lots of room. There are cargo holds, shuttles and a large bridge. Even the ceilings are high enough for a human. Besides, I'd enjoy having you as a member of my crew."

I ask, "Felicia, you have a crew? Are there more cats like you on the ship?" She responds, "In the early days, the space authority on Meowmax sent out individual small sized cats, like me, on long sub light speed trips. I was put in stasis during the years it took to get to your system. Now it takes only days to get here so the space program was opened to the other feline species on Meowmax."

I say, "What kind of species are you talking about?" Felicia says, "One is bigger than me. My first officer, Leo, resemble an Earth tiger, but human size." I say, "Really? Tigers? Anything else that I should know about before I make my decision?" Felicia says, "This mission is deliberately intended to be a cooperative effort by multiple species, including ones that are alien to Meowmax. In the last few decades, we have encountered other intelligent species within and near the Proxima Centauri system. One species is similar in appearance to a small dinosaur species of pre-historic Earth. They look scary, but really are quite nice. Also, we have recruited a few other species that we encountered during our initial exploration of other planets, moons and asteroids. My crew is quite a collection of aliens."

I'm both dumbfounded and at the same time excited by what Felicia has proposed. My cute furry friend is the captain of an interstellar starship, and she wants me to join her merry crew of aliens. I could become the first human to venture beyond our solar system. How can I turn the opportunity down?

Over the next hour Felicia provides me with more information about her mission. She confirms that she is the captain of the Starkitty1. The faster than light, portal technology is authorized for travel within the specific quadrant of the Milky Way galaxy where Meowmax and Earth reside. That is an area of about 100 light years wide and about 100 light years long. This is a small portion of the galaxy, but it does contain millions of stars and planetary systems to explore. If I agree to go with Felicia, I will be trained in all aspects of ship's operations. This includes propulsion, life support, navigation, communications and weapons. I ask Felicia why we would need weapons? I ask, "Isn't this a peaceful mission of exploration?" She replies, "We really do not know what to expect from the species we encounter on the planets that we will be exploring. Yes, our mission is peaceful. The weapons we have on board will be used exclusively for defensive purposes if the ship is attacked."

I'm really getting excited now. All I can think of saying is, "Beam me up Scotty!" I tell Felicia that space travel has been my dream ever since I met her. I accept her proposal. I'm going back into space!

In preparation for leaving Earth, I tell my friends and family that I will be away for a long time traveling around the world. I tell them that I will be off the grid and out of cell phone range. Of course, they will have no idea how far off the grid I will be!

The Starkitty1

Felicia gave me a communicator and a universal language translator so that I can communicate with my new shipmates once I board the ship. She also asks me to take three days to wrap up my personal affairs on Earth.

Three days later I am sitting on the same bench at Shoreline Park. I'm still blown away by the whole idea of going on an intra galactic adventure. Felicia suddenly materializes next to me. I ask her how the transporter works. "Does a body deconstruct on one end and then somehow reconstruct on the other end?" She says, "Billy, this is not Star Trek. We don't have an actual transporter. We utilize a scaled down version of the same portal technology that is used to move our ship through great distances. First, I locate the coordinates of the destination where I want to go. Then I open a small portal. I can see the destination through the portal. Finally, I step through the portal and voila! Here I am!" I ask, "So, is that how we will get back on your ship?" Felicia responds, "Correct!"

Felicia asks me if I am ready to board the Starkitty1. I am nervous because this could possibly be the last moment that I stand on planet Earth. After some thought, I reply, "I'm ready." Felicia meows a command into the communicator located on her collar. In an instant, a portal opens in front of us. On the other side I see an empty room. She turns to me and says, "One small step for Billy. One great step for mankind!" I step into the portal. On the other side I'm in a room, facing the bare wall. Felicia is standing next to me. I hear a voice behind me saying, "Grrr, welcome back captain Felicia. I see you have brought a friend with you. This must be the human that you call Billy."

I slowly turn around and find myself facing two cats about the same size as Felicia, a human sized tiger and two creatures that look like the velociraptors from the Jurassic Park movies. My jaw drops. For a moment, I'm speechless. The tiger says, "Grrr, what's the matter Billy? Cats got your tongue?" This quip elicits a round of laughter from everyone including myself. One of the raptors says, "Leo, you're killing me!" More laughter ensues. I'm getting the impression that this is a real fun bunch of aliens.

I introduce myself, "Hi everyone, my name is Billy Wilson. You can call me Billy." I'm getting the impression that last names don't matter here. The tiger responds that his name is Leo. One raptor introduces herself as Tara. The other raptor is a male named Rex. They both smile. I can see that each has a full mouth filled with large, sharp teeth. The two cats introduce themselves next. One is a black longhaired cat named Milo. The other is a gray Siamese named Bella. Felicia chimes in that there is another crewmember crawling about, "He resembles a giant spider. His name is Skip. Try not to trip over Skip while navigating the corridors. Skip is prone to taking short naps pretty much anywhere on the ship. He may even be hanging on a wall or ceiling. Skip specializes in doing maintenance. He can easily squeeze into spaces that are difficult for the rest of the crewmembers to access." Then she says, "There is also Jess, a recent addition to the crew. Jess is around here somewhere too. More on Jess later.

I say, "Wow, this is all pretty new stuff for me." Tara comments, "It was the same for each of us when we agreed to join this mission. There was a lot to get used to living with aliens from other worlds, but Felicia makes sure that everyone on the ship feels at ease. She is a super captain!"

Leo says, "Grrr, Billy, I can show you to your quarters. We watched some episodes of Fixer Upper and This Old House. Then we fixed up one of the quarters to suit the needs of a human. Our food replicators are also programmed with a menu from Nobu, McDonalds, Taco Bell, KFC, Panda Express and a few other popular restaurants. I hope you like the selection. The food replicator system can be tweaked if the food taste is a bit off." I reply, "Leo, I'm sure that I will love it. Thanks for all you have done to make me feel comfortable."

As Leo leads me down a corridor, he says, we have the ship on a daily time cycle of approximately twenty-six and a half of your Earth hours. This seems to work out for the felines and raptors. I think that it will probably work out for you too. The only exceptions are Skip and Jess. Skip will nod off at any time and Jess does not sleep.

Leo stops in front of a door and places his right paw on the pad next to it. The door opens. He enters the room and beckons me to follow him. Once inside he points out some of the amenities in the room. There is a table with four chairs around it. The chairs have height adjustments to accommodate a range of alien body types. Then he says, "Grrr, the only one who does not need a chair is Skip. When we have meetings or activities, Skip prefers to hang from the ceiling."

Next, Leo shows me a countertop extending out of the wall. At the far end is a wall-mounted dispenser with a keypad and video screen next to it. He says, "Grrr, you can either type in your food or drink selection or use the touch screen to select a picture of the standard items. Leo gives me a demonstration on how to do a food selection. He tells me that I can even try out some raptor or feline selections. Then I notice a section with pictures of various insects and bugs. I ask Leo, "Who is that for?" Leo replies, "Grrr, it's for Skip. He is particularly fond of the synthetic fly and moth selections. Not my favorites though." Leo goes on to say that there is a selection of fruit. The raptors are particularly fond of apples, grapes and berries. When we added them to the menu, they were very happy about it."

Leo continues, "Grrr, you can use voice commands to request a selection of Earth music. Skip is particularly adept at hacking. He got into the Apple Music library and downloaded a selection of classical, bluegrass, soul, rap, rock and pop music. I like Nirvana and Cold Play. I must say that you humans have good musical taste. Raptor music is not for me. Too many screeching and chomping sounds! And Skip's music is just a series of scratching sounds. To each his own I guess!"

Leo moves to another part of the room. He says, "Grrr, the ship's computer interface is over here. You can interface with the computer via a keypad, mouse, voice or touchscreen. In the folder titled 'Manuals For Billy' are some tutorials describing the critical onboard systems that Felicia wants you to study. They have all been translated into Earth English. Once you complete each tutorial, one of us will take you for hands-on training. Felicia insists that each crewmember learn how to operate all the ship's critical systems."

Then I ask Leo about how gravity is created on the ship. During my Mars mission, we astronauts spent a lot of time floating around in zero gravity. On the Starkitty1, I feel firmly planted on the deck of the ship. How is that possible? Leo explains that in the early days of space exploration, the first ships operated with zero gravity. That was ok for shorter missions.

Later, a rotating ship design was created for longer trips between planets in the Proxima Centauri solar system. The rotation created centrifugal force, which provided an effect like gravity. Meanwhile, our scientists were working on technologies to create artificial gravity for longer haul trips. About the same time that they made the breakthrough with portal technology, they also perfected a gravity simulator. That technology is being used on the Starkitty1. Leo comments that the Starkitty1 has a gravity that is about eighty-three percent that of Earth. It is a level that seems to work ok for all the crewmembers. Their home planets have varying levels of gravity due to differing mass. I tell Leo that explains why I have felt light on my feet since arriving on the ship.

Leo continues demonstrating equipment features in my quarters for another thirty minutes. Then he departs. A few minutes later a buzzer sounds. I figure that someone must be at the door. So, I walk over and look at the video display that shows the corridor in front of my quarters. Nobody is standing outside my door. But I can hear a strange scratching sound. I open the door and come face to face with six blinking eyes in an upside-down face. I'm startled, so my immediate reaction is to jump backwards. I look up and see a huge spider hanging upside down from the corridor ceiling. It has a large round body and eight thick furry legs. A round head protrudes from the front with six eyes and an almost human looking mouth.

The spider begins speaking. "Hi, I'm Skip, sorry to have startled you. That's the same reaction that the raptors had when they first set their eyes on me. Of course, it also took a while for me to get used to them too. Maybe it will be easier for you if I'm standing on the floor." Skip crawls down the wall and onto the floor. He says, "May I come in?" By now, I have regained my composure and in a somewhat shaky voice say, "Sure Skip, come on in."

Skip walks in and looks around. He says, "Nice place you have here. Is the sound system working?" I say, "Yes, Leo says it should work, but I haven't tried it out yet." Skip says, "Mind if I give it a whirl?" I say, "Go ahead." Skip says, "Play Arachnoid Rhapsody Number Three." The audio system begins playing a series of clicks and hisses. Skip starts dancing and swaying to the sounds. He says, "That music just reaches down into my soul every time I hear it!" After a while, Skip notices that I am just standing there with my jaw dropped. He says, "Oh, sorry, I just got a bit carried away with the music." Then he says, "Music stop!" The music goes silent. Skip says, "And now for the purpose of my visit. First, I want to personally welcome you to the Starkitty1. You are the first human that I have encountered. I'm here to give you a quick tour of the ship. Is this a good time for you?" I reply that it's as good a time as any. Skip says, "Ok, then let's start. Is it all right if I move along on the ceiling? I prefer that position. You know, more blood flowing to the brain."

The first stop is the break room. "This is where we come to relax, get a drink and talk to our fellow crewmates. It's particularly fun when Leo is here. He's a real crack up. Leo always has a story or a joke to share with us." Skip then tries to imitate Leo by saying "Grrr! Do you know what the panther said to the lion?" Then he emits a series of high-pitched clicking noises. I can only assume that he is laughing at his impersonation of Leo.

We move on down to the next room. This room is much larger. It has two tables and several bays with touch screens on the walls next to them. Skip says, "This is our recreation and workout room. You just make a selection on the touch screen and the machine you selected is pushed out into the bay. When you are done, the machine will push back into the wall. We have machines configured for the various aliens on this ship." He returns to the tables and says, "We sometimes gather here to play cards and other games of chance. Yes, one thing in common for aliens is that we all like to gamble every now and then. I usually hang from the ceiling and make sure nobody is cheating!" I say, "Really? Aliens cheat at cards? Who knew?"

In the corner is a small plunge pool that is covered up right now. Skip says, "One thing that we all have in common is that we enjoy a dip in fresh water from time to time. Even the feline members of the crew enjoy a dip in the pool. Just push the button and the cover retracts. The cover is a precaution for when we are doing some intense maneuvering. We don't want water spilled everywhere."

The propulsion room is where the sub-light speed photon drive is located. "We used the photon drive when we are near planets or other objects, and we need to make precise maneuvers. Otherwise, we use the portal generator for the large distance jumps. Photon drive is limited by the speed of light, so it takes a long time to travel any significant distance in space. The portal generator is good for a jump of many light years distance in an instant. It turns out to be a simple device compared to a photon drive. The portal generator is kept inside a console in on the bridge."

Skip tells me that it's now time to go to the bridge. On our way we encounter a thing that looks like a rolling blob of material coming the other way. I ask

Skip, "Who or what is that?" Skip says, "Oh we must have forgotten to tell you about Jess. Jess is a shape shifting entity. Jess can observe an object by studying its contours. Then Jess will take on the shape of the object. Jess can also imitate the appearance of beings. Jess helps me with ship maintenance from time to time due to her ability to change into a liquid and ooze into hard-to-reach places that I cannot access. One other thing that we discovered is that Jess has some sort of magical healing power. If you have a cut or break a bone, Jess can help fix the injury fast."

Skip stops and greets Jess, he says, "Hey Jess! I hope that you are having a good day! I'd like you to meet our newest crewmember, Billy. Billy is a human." Jess stops. A portion of Jess's body forms into a head with two eyes and a mouth. Jess says, "Pleased to meet you, Billy. Welcome to the Starkitty1! You are going to like it here. Everyone is very nice."

At this point I have seen so many strange things that Jess fits right in. I say, "Pleased to meet you, Jess." Jess reverts to blob form and proceeds past us down the corridor." I ask Skip, "Is Jess a male or female entity?" Skip responds, "I'm not sure. Gender really does not seem to apply to Jess. But Jess is quite entertaining at times. With all the transformations, I mean. If you see an object that is a little out of place, it could be Jess! Usually there is a small mistake in detail. I have become good at spotting Jess. Jess is good at card games too. Jess can extend multiple arms and shuffle several card decks at once. For that reason, Jess is always our card dealer." I reply, "So among other things, Jess is the ship's entertainer?" Skip says, "You could say that. We play a lot of cards in our leisure time!"

We reach the end of the corridor and enter the bridge. Felicia is sitting in the captain's chair. Also, there are Tara on communications and Rex at the navigation console. Felicia turns towards Skip and I and says, "Billy, welcome to the bridge!" Tara and Rex both say, "Hi Billy!" Felicia then points to the large transparent window. It wraps around the bridge, providing more than 180 degrees of visibility. The view is spectacular. The Earth is in plain view. I say, "Wow! What material is that window made of?" Felicia says, "It's a solid structural material that appears transparent. Sensors mounted around the outside of the ship feed visual information to a coating on the inside surface of the hull that encases the bridge. It creates the illusion of being transparent." Then Felicia continues saying, "How do you like the Starkitty1? I reply, "Felicia, this ship is awesome. I keep pinching myself expecting to wake up from this dream, but I'm still here!"

Tara says, "It was the same for me. Back on our home planet of Trexia, Rex and I worked as test pilots. We were piloting one of the first space capsules on a course towards a nearby moon. That capsule was nothing like the Starkitty1. In fact, both Rex and I are lucky to even be here. Our navigation system had a malfunction that put us seriously off course. We were flying out into open space at maximum velocity. Our communications with Trexia cut out. We sent a distress signal. The signal was getting weaker and weaker. We were rationing our food but then it ran out. Life support was failing. We thought that it was the end for us."

Rex cuts in to say, "I recall being cold and barely breathing. Then I remember total darkness. I thought that this must be death. After a time, I could feel myself lying down on a soft surface. I felt weak and my vision was blurry. I could hear voices but could not make out what they were saying. I passed out again and slept. Was I in the afterlife?" Rex pauses, "I woke up again to see two furry faces gazing down at me. They both had a kind look in their eyes. It was Felicia and Leo looking down at me."

Tara says, "The Starkitty1 detected our distress signal and found our capsule traveling aimlessly in space. When they boarded the capsule, they found us barely alive. They brought us on board the Starkitty1. We have been here ever since. They saved us."

Rex says, "Felicia offered to take us home to Trexia, but we decided that we wanted to stay on the

Starkitty1. So, we sent a message back to Trexia to let them know that we were well and off on a space adventure."

Felicia says, "Tara and Rex have become valued members of the crew. In fact, all the crewmembers have been making valuable contributions. Even Jess."

I ask Felicia, "Where are we going next? She points her paw at the stars in the viewing window. She says, "Out there!"

Felicia

Felicia has returned to the quarters that she shares with Milo and Bella. Felines of Meowmax are a communal species and like to live in groups. There are cushions spread all around Felicia's living quarters. These can be used as a place to relax or sleep. Right now, she is alone and thinking about the journey that her life has taken to get to where she is today.

As a kitten, she always dreamed of travelling to the stars. She would go outside and stare at the night's sky. She wondered about what kinds of worlds existed out there. How many of them supported life? If so, was there intelligent life on those worlds? Were the worlds populated by felines? Or were there other intelligent life forms on those worlds? On Meowmax there are numerous intelligent species of felines. There are the cats like her, panthers, lions and the tigers. The tigers make up the core of the Meowmax scientific community. The cats initially tended to go into the space program due to their small size. Sub-light space travel required small ships. The cats were best suited for that role. With the discovery of portal technology, that all changed. Soon any feline species could join the space program.

Felicia studied the sciences, astronomy and astrophysics in school. She was at the top of her class and applied for the space program upon graduation from advanced studies. She passed her exams and the physical fitness requirements to become an astronaut. She went on a few short missions inside the Proxima Centauri system before being selected for a mission to the nearby Earth solar system. Of course, that meant being put into stasis for four years each way due to the long passage of time required for the mission. This is when Felicia met Billy on planet Earth. After leaving the Earth solar system, she thought about Billy a lot. She suspected that their paths would cross again someday. It turned out that she was right about that.

So here she is, fulfilling her dreams. She departed Meowmax with a capable crew of Leo, Milo, Bella and Skip. Along the way she added the raptors, Tara and Rex. Then came Jess and finally Billy. So far, everyone has fit in. The felines of Meowmax are a tolerant species. They are accepting of other species regardless of superficial differences. For example, no two cats on Meowmax look the same. There are various breeds with a variety of size and color differences. Everyone has a place in feline society. This made it easy for Felicia to look beyond the superficial characteristics of an alien species and focus on the character of each individual. Maybe that is why she likes Billy so much. He is smart, thoughtful and kind.

Felicia's thoughts are interrupted when Milo and Bella walk into the quarters. They join Felicia on the cushion. The cats follow their traditional social greeting by touch noses. Then they begin grooming each other. This is a favorite communal activity for felines. Even after a good swim in the pool, there is always time for grooming. Soon they all curl up together and have a catnap. Occasionally Leo will join them. That's why the cushions in her quarters are all extra-large.

The Crew

I have been on the ship for three weeks now. The training has been very intense so far. There is a lot to learn about the Starkitty1's systems. So far, I am trained in life support and communications. Next, I will be studying the operation of the photon drive propulsion system and the portal projector. The last thing that I will be trained on will be the weapon systems and piloting a shuttle.

I have been issued a skintight smart suit that features a built-in environmental control, universal translator and communicator. The suit responds to both verbal and thought communications. I started out with verbal communications because that is what I am most familiar with. The thought communications will take a lot more getting used to. Humans tend to be a little more scatter brained than raptors, felines and spiders. Everyone is wearing a smart suit, even the cats. On Earth, Felicia never wore clothing, but here, she dresses like a proper ship captain.

Leo and Skip have been my principal trainers. Both are patient and take their time to explain things. My previous training experience at NASA has helped me a lot. My mind was already wired to digest a huge amount of information. Even though everyone is trained on all systems, some do have a specialty. Skip is the electronics and mechanical expert. Leo is Felicia's first officer and understands how all the systems play together. Tara, Rex, Milo and Bella spend much of their time with communications and navigation. Milo and Bella also specialize as shuttle pilots. There are four shuttles of various sizes in the Starkitty1's cargo bays. The one used most frequently is the Fastcat2.

On the surface, Jess's principal talent appears to be dealing cards. Later I discover that Jess's shape shifting ability is indispensable at critical times. Jess can survive in any environmental condition, even in open space. This is because Jess does not need to breath or eat. Jess simply exists. Jess does not get sick nor does Jess age. Jess can also heal injuries. I begin to wonder, *"Do we have an immortal being among us?"*

When I asked Felicia how she met Jess, she said that on one of its first missions, the Starkitty1 was assigned to explore a passing comet. The Starkitty1 was projected in close to the comet. The Fastcat2 shuttle was launched from the Starkitty1. Its mission was to land the comet's surface and gather data. Milo was the pilot. While walking around on the surface of the comet, Milo observed a rock that appeared to be changing shapes. He watched the shape shifting rock for a while but then decided to return to the shuttle. When Milo opened the shuttle door, the shape shifting rock slipped past him and climbed in. Milo was unsure what to make of the situation. It appeared that the shape shifter wanted to stay in the shuttle rather than return to the comet. Milo was not sure what to do next, so he asked Felicia for guidance. Felicia told Milo to bring the shape shifter back to the Starkitty1. After passing through decontamination, the shape shifter just started wandering around and changing into common objects on the ship. Leo named the shape shifter, Jess after a magical feline from Meowmax fantasy literature. In time Jess was able to form a face and developed speech. Jess exhibited an amazing ability to absorb information and adapt to life on the ship. Jess has been a valued member of the crew ever since. Over time, Jess has become knowledge about all the ship's operations.

Felicia is the glue that holds our merry band of aliens together. She is the final authority when a decision must be made. Having said that, she readily asks us for council before making decisions. She is unquestionably our leader.

Skip is also somewhat of a mystery. He had been a traveler on a spaceship that crash-landed on Felicia's home planet of Meowmax. Some nearby felines were able to rescue Skip from the wreckage. After some effort, Skip's language was added to the universal translator program. It was learned that Skip was a crewmember on a multi-generational spaceship that was launched from his home system hundreds of years ago. The ship was damaged in a collision with an asteroid and lost much of its propulsion capability. The captain decided to land the ship on Meowmax because there was evidence of an advanced space traveling civilization who could perhaps help them repair the ship. The landing turned into a crash, and all were lost except for Skip. Skip had been born on the ship and was unaware of the exact location of his home planet. Skip also did not know the ultimate destination of the ship.

The cats of Meowmax were very accepting of Skip and found that he had an aptitude for electronics, mechanics and programming. Skip asked to become part of the Meowmax space program. The feline leadership agreed. When Felicia met Skip, she was very impressed. She asked for him to be part of her Starkitty1 crew.

First Mission - Europa

We have been traveling at sub-light speed towards the planet, Jupiter. Felicia calls us together. She tells us that Jupiter is a planet that has quite a few interesting looking moons. Several could harbor life. She singles out the moon, Europa. "Our sensors indicate that Europa has an ice crust. Below the crust there appears to be an ocean of water. Leo proposes that we have the Starkitty1 hover over the ice crust and then project a shuttle into the ocean using the portal projector. Milo comments that the shuttles navigate in water just as easily as in space, so there should be no problem exploring the sub-surface ocean. Leo recommends that we should first send a probe into the ocean to make sure that it is safe for a shuttle. I'm so excited by this first mission. I remember studying Jupiter and the Jovian moons in college astronomy. There was much speculation about what we would find there some day. Now I'm going to have a chance to see what is there. I immediately volunteer to ride in a shuttle. Felicia says, "You can ride with me and Milo on the Fastcat2." I'm overwhelmed with emotion. I say, "Thanks Felicia."

The Starkitty1 is approaching the Jupiter system. The rings are clearly visible. As we get closer, the moons of Jupiter come into view. The first to become visible are Callisto and Ganymede. Then Io and Europa come into view. Jupiter now appears as a giant striped ball. The storm that forms the giant red eye is enormous. Felicia tells Tara to navigate the Starkitty1 so that it is hovering over Europa's ice crust.

Felicia, Milo and I walk over to the cargo bay where the Fastcat2 shuttle is located. Next to it are two-dozen small probes. Felicia activates one of the probes and projects it into the ocean just below Europa's crust. A display on the wall of the shuttle bay is showing the various views that the probe is sending back to the ship. Instruments are measuring the chemical content of the water as well as water temperature, currents and other relevant data. Felicia relays the data to Tara, Rex and Leo. They all agree that it is ok to project the Fastcat2 into the ocean of Europa. The probe relays back projection coordinates for the shuttle. Tara downloads the coordinates into the shuttle computer. Felicia smiles at me and says, "It's a go!"

Felicia meows and the sliding door on the shuttle opens. We enter the shuttle and walk over to the control console. It has been configured with cat-sized seats for Milo and Felicia. There is a human sized seat for me. The shuttle has a big window in the front and several display screens showing views from all sides of the shuttle. We sit in the seats and strap in. Felicia meows' commands into the console. A portal opens in front of us. The Fastcat2 rises and passes through the portal into Europa's sub-ice ocean.

We are suspended in the ocean. Above us is the blue of Europa's ice crust. Surprisingly, the ocean is illuminated. Something is generating the light. The instruments are detecting tiny florescent microorganisms floating in the water. The microorganisms appear to be the source of the light. I recall that scientists back on Earth have said that where there is water, there is life. In the case of Europa, they are dead on. I'm wondering what other life we will find here. Something must feed on these microorganisms.

Felicia looks at Milo and says, "Let's do this!" The Fastcat2 begins moving slowly through the water. Felicia says, "Look at that ahead of us!" She magnifies the screen. I can see a large underground vent that is spewing gas up from the ocean floor. There appears to be a pocket of gas collecting under the ice crust. I say, "Can we get a closer look? I'll bet that there are more vents down there. If we find vents, we may find life around the vents." Milo steers the shuttle towards the base of gas flume. Felicia comments that the instruments are detecting an area of high geothermal activity just ahead. "Billy, I think we found a center of life here in the ocean." The cameras are showing multiple vents that are expressing gas into the ocean. Swarming around the vents are millions of small creatures ranging from short thin filaments to creatures resembling shrimp. The temperature in the ocean is very cold, but as we approach the vents, the temperature rises quickly. Felicia comments, "Life is non-existent on the surface of Europa due intense cold and radiation from Jupiter. But down here under a thick layer of ice and a deep ocean, we have all the building blocks necessary for life to flourish."

Leo calls in over the communication channel. He says that he has been monitoring the ice crust above our location. The ice is about two miles thick which is thinner than the crust covering most or Europa. The crust also appears to have deep fissures in it. Periodically, there are bursts of hot water vapor erupting from the fissures. These eruptions are quite spectacular. The water vapor is spewed hundreds of miles out into space. Felicia responds that this is likely caused by the pressure buildup of the gas emitted from the vents on the ocean floor. She sends Leo images of the sea life that is flourishing around the vents.

We are observing one particularly active vent when something unexpected occurs. A long, thin, needle shaped creature winds through the water towards the vent, opens its mouth and ingests many of the shrimp creatures. Then it swims away and disappears from our view. I comment to Felicia, "Looks like we found the next level predator." I say, "I wonder what else we will find if we keep looking around here. These vents probably contain creatures that are at the bottom of the food chain. Higher level predators will likely stop by at one time or another for a meal."

Sure enough, while we are monitoring the vents, another predator creature swims by. It is about the size of a salmon and with sharp teeth, it is almost transparent. When it zooms in to scoop up some shrimp, we can see the swallowed shrimp inside its body.

A while later an even larger predator visits the vent. We notice that the larger predators all have sharp teeth. It begs the question as to why? We will soon find out.

After spending considerable time observing the vents and collecting data, we move on. Felicia tells Milo to navigate along the bottom of the seabed because this appears to be where the life is concentrated. We occasionally pass over a large swimming creature and yet other creatures that resemble Earth crabs. Always we observe sharp claws or teeth on these creatures. I postulate that there must be some fierce competition for survival among the predators. Then, while we are passing over a large hole in the sea floor, a giant serpentine head bolts out of the hole and wraps its body around the shuttle. The creature begins shaking the shuttle violently as it tries to draw it back into the hole. Thankfully we are all seated and strapped in, or we would have been thrown into the walls of the shuttle. Nonetheless, we are quite startled by this turn of events. We can see the gray body of the creature through the shuttle windows. Milo says, "Hold on!" Then he guns the engines of the shuttle. The force of our acceleration causes the creature to be pulled out of the hole, but it has not yet let go. Felicia says, "This creature is a tough sucker." Milo turns the shuttle violently to the left and then to the right. The creature finally let's go. We look back at the creature and observe that it is very long, and snake like in structure. Having failed to capture our shuttle. The creature begins to pull its body back into the hole. Then it disappears entirely. Leo's voice comes over the communication interface. He asks, "Grrr, are you all ok? From the video feed, it appeared that some sort of giant sea creature grabbed a hold of the shuttle." Felicia responds, "We are all safe. It really gave us a violent shaking and tried to pull us into its lair. Milo gunned our engines and it eventually let go. That's why it's always a good idea to be strapped into your seat. You never know what can happen next." I speculate that if a predator is this huge and powerful, its prey must also be very large.

As we proceed along, we are staying a little farther away whenever we detect large holes in the seabed. We are now using our longer distance sensors to detect large moving objects. We are also to monitoring the sea floor topology for areas that could contain the huge snake creature that attacked us. This provides a more accurate map of what is ahead of the Fastcat2. The sensors pick up a pod of large creatures approaching from behind us. There are eight creatures in the pod, and they are about the size of an Earth Orca. Their approach speed is surprisingly fast for creatures of their size. Felicia tells Milo to let them get close to us so she can get closeup video and study their predatory behavior.

The video display is providing a closeup view of the creatures. They have thick bodies that are about thirty feet long and have long powerful tails that provide their propulsion through the water. Fins on both sides of their bodies help them steer. They have large mouths full of sharp teeth. A gill like organ on each side of their body likely performs a respiratory function. These creatures have all the markings of an apex predator. What is of particular interest is their ability to communicate between themselves using sounds as they pursue a prey. Felicia activates the universal translator. She is hoping that the translator can read the sounds the creatures are making and translate them. In moments, a stream of translations can be heard.

The creatures refer to each other as distinct individuals. The creature at the front of the pod appears to be the leader. The pod of eight creatures is in pack hunting mode and has mistaken the Fastcat2 to be a creature that it preys on. The lead creature has given instructions to the other members of the pod to surround the Fastcat2. Some of the communications between individual creatures are, up, down, left, right, fast, slow. Each time that Milo slows the Fastcat2 down and lets the pod catch up, they also slow down and try to surround the ship. Then Milo bursts out of the trap and the creatures resume the pursuit. After a few failed attempts at capturing the Fastcat2, the leader turns away. The translator picks up the word "Not." The other creatures follow the leader. They repeat the word "Not!" to each other." Felicia says, "The leader realized that this pursuit is a waste of time. I believe that they figured out that we are not prey worth pursuing.

I tell Felicia, "The Europa ocean appears to be a dangerous place to explore if one is not prepared. There are some dangerous predators lurking about." Felicia agrees. Then she says, "Billy, I hope you enjoyed your first mission." I say, "It was the best!" Felicia says, "Time to return to the Starkitty1." In moments, we have passed through a portal and are safely back in the shuttlecraft bay. Leo, Bella and Tara are there to greet us. Felicia asks Leo, "What happened to the probe. Is it still in the ocean? Leo responds, "Grrr, it got munched by one of those creatures that was chasing your shuttle. We are getting great video of the inside of the creature!" Milo quips, "If we wait around long enough, the creature may poop it out!"

Bella says, "Funny!"

Relaxing

The Starkitty1 has finished its exploration of Jupiter and the Jovian moons. Leo lets us all know that we can take a break now before the ship makes the portal jump to our next destination, Saturn. Felicia tells everyone that they have free time to engage in recreational activities for the next few time cycles. Tara puts the Starkitty1 on autopilot. For now, the ship will be flying through open space at sub light speed.

I'm eager to see what my shipmates do during their downtime, so I head over to the recreation room. I hope to get in a workout and maybe a dip in the pool. I'm walking down the corridor and pass under Skip, who is hanging from the ceiling. Skip appears to be in a dormant state, so I do not disturb him. I know from my college studies that spiders have irregular sleep patterns. Skip may be following a similar pattern. Or it may be that this is how Skip relaxes.

I enter the recreation room and see Tara and Rex on two of the treadmills. Initially the conversation I hear between them is a series of hisses and guttural noises. When I get closer, the universal translator kicks in and I can understand most of what they are saying. Tara greets me, "Hi Billy, are you here for a workout?" I respond, "Yeah, I'm trying to stay in shape. Maybe I'll start by working out on an elliptical."

To my right is an empty exercise bay. I walk over to the touch screen on the wall and sort through the equipment selections offered until I find the human elliptical. I touch the image. A moment later a door in the wall opens. I can hear the conveyor system behind the wall running until it locates the selected elliptical machine. Then it pushes it out into the exercise bay. This is really an awesome system!

So now I'm on the elliptical beginning my workout when I notice a change in the room. When I walked in, there was a bench in one corner of the room. Now I see that there is a table in its place. I ask Tara if she noticed the change? Tara replies, "Oh, it's just Jess messing around doing the shape shifting thing. Apparently, this is how Jess exercises. In a moment Jess may change into something else."

Sure enough, the table turns in to an undulating blob and then forms into a chair. I comment, "Jess, that's pretty impressive." A blob begins to rise out of the seat of the chair. Then the blob forms into mouth. The lips on the mouth begin to move and say, "Thanks for the complement, Billy!" Then the mouth recedes back into the blob and the blob recedes into the chair seat. Needless to say, I'm pretty blown away by Jess's quick changes.

I continue with my workout, on the elliptical and watch Jess go through a progression of changes. First Jess changes into a lamp, followed by a computer keyboard and then a display screen. Jess is really entertaining.

After my workout, I decide to take a dip in the pool. I go to the control panel and push the button to retract the cover. That being done, I step into the pool. It's rather small so it only takes eight strokes of freestyle before I reach the far side of the pool. After a few laps, I see Bella enter the recreation room. She greets Tara, Rex, Jess and Myself. Then she walks over to one of the bays and selects her exercise equipment. The door opens and an apparatus emerges. The apparatus could be described as a miniature treadmill perfectly sized for Bella. Bella steps onto the treadmill. She meows an instruction. Immediately the treadmill surface begins moving. I can barely contain myself to see this cute ball of fur trotting along on the treadmill surface. I must remind myself that I in the recreation room of an alien spaceship, not my local YMCA.

I go back to swimming laps when Felicia walks up to the pool and says hello. She says, "Mind if I join you?" I say, "Sure, there's plenty of room." Felicia jumps into a pool and begins paddling back and forth using all fours. I switch to breaststroke just so that I can watch her do laps. Felicia is a pretty good swimmer. I'm surprised that a cat can move so quickly through the water. Again, I must remind myself that Felicia is not an Earth cat. I later learn that back in her formative years on Meowmax, Felicia was a championship swimmer.

A few minutes later, Milo shows up and joins us in the pool. Bella joins us too. So, I'm in a swimming pool with three wet cats and everyone is having a good time splashing around.

I'm done swimming so I grab a towel and head to the shower room. Apparently, there are no private showers on this ship. Everyone has a lax attitude about nudity anyway so here I am, naked and taking a shower with cats and raptors of both genders. It takes a bit of getting used to at first, but after a week, I don't even think about it anymore.

I find myself in my quarters lying on the bed and relaxing after a good workout. Leo's voice comes on over the intercom. He says, "There will be a card game starting up shortly in the break room. Jess will be dealing blackjack. I'm thinking, "Alien blackjack? Dealt by a shape shifter no less. I can't miss this!" So, I get dressed up and walk to the break room. I see that the table is already set. There are eight seats. Skip is hanging from the ceiling and Jess has taken the form of a female Las Vegas card dealer with three sets of hands. Jess reaches under the table with one set of hands and pulls up a box. Inside the box are chips. With incredible speed, Jess's hands go to work building up even sized piles of chips on the table, in front of each of the seven chairs. Then Jess pulls three decks of cards from the box. Each of Jess's three sets of hands begins shuffling a deck of cards. When Jess is done shuffling the three decks, they are combined into one large deck. Jess places the large deck into a dealing shoe. Then Jess looks at me and winks her right eye. I must admit that I am touched by the gesture. There is really something compelling about Jess.

While this has been going on, my shipmates begin filing into the room and taking their places around the table. Felicia looks at me and says, "Ever since we entered your solar system, we have been playing Earth games of chance. We downloaded some instructional videos and watched them. Jess caught on quickly to the dealer's role in the games. You can see that Jess is pretty good at shuffling cards." I say, "No kidding." Felicia continues, "Jess is good at dealing Poker and Baccarat too. I comment, "If Jess ever gets bored of space travel, Jess could make a pretty good living in Las Vegas."

Felicia looks up at Skip and says, "Skip does not play cards but loves to watch us. With Skip watching over us, there is no cheating." Then she says, "The chips have no monetary value. There is nothing to buy on the ship, but it is fun to see who ends up with the most chips at the end of the session. Usually, Jess ends up with the biggest pile of chips when we play blackjack because Jess is the house. Leo is pretty good at card counting so he often has the next biggest pile of chips.

Everyone is seated now. Jess has retained the form of a female card dealer, and an attractive one at that. I'm thinking, maybe Jess is a female after all. Jess says, "Blackjack pays 3 to 2. Splitting is allowed. Ties result in a push. Bust over 21." Jess begins dealing the cards. My first hand is a pair of aces. I decide to split them. Leo is particularly interested in how I play my hand. Apparently, none of my crewmates have experimented with splitting their hands. Jess deals me a ten on one and a king on the other. Two blackjacks! I say, "Beginners luck!" Jess pays me immediately. Leo says, "Grrr, impressive! I'm going to have to study the odds for splitting."

After about forty hands of blackjack, we switch to poker. At this point in the session, Leo has the most chips of the players. I'm really interested to see if any of the aliens will be bluffing. I wonder what a 'poker face' looks like on a raptor or a cat? I find out soon enough. Apparently, Tara is very good at providing blank expressions when she has a potentially winning hand. Leo is pretty good too. Felicia, Milo and Bella will often give themselves away by meowing as soon as they receive a good card. Rex is pretty good at bluffing too, but not as good as Tara.

After about two and a half hours of playing cards, we all agree that we have had enough. The grand winner is Tara, followed by Leo. We all had a good time and are about to head back to our quarters when Felicia reminds us that we will be doing some martial arts self-defense training during the next time cycle. I'm thinking, "How do cats and raptors do martial arts? I can't wait to see this!"

I'm in my room now and about to doze off. I'm thinking about the many turns that my life has taken. Things were going along normally for a kid my age when I was in high school. I was an average student who played one sport but was otherwise unremarkable. I did not have a girlfriend. I did not know what I was going to do with myself after high school. Then I met Felicia. That changed everything. I realized that I wanted to become like her, traveling out in space and visiting other worlds. I wanted to become an astronaut. I now had a dream and worked my butt off to achieve it. I earned a doctorate in astrophysics at UC Berkeley. Then I succeeded in becoming an astronaut and flying to Mars. All the while, my personal life was put on hold. Now I am here, traveling to planets that no other human will likely visit for hundreds of years, if ever.

Then I wonder, if I ever return back to Earth, what will I say to other people when they ask me where I have spent the last few years? How do I explain all of this? I saw what the reaction was when I tried to tell the NASA investigators about Felicia. They will think that I went nuts! Oh well, maybe I'm just worrying too much? I decide to enjoy the ride and not worry about what may follow later. After another few minutes I fall off into a deep sleep.

Alien Martial Arts

The martial arts session was a real trip! We started with thirty minutes of basic exercises, strikes, blocks and kicks (For those who could kick). Then we went on to some sparring. This posed some interesting questions. How does a cat spar with a tiger? The size difference is so great. Well, the answer is to run and find a weapon or two friends to help you! It's a bit of a mismatch. The three cats tried to gang up on Leo. Leo had no problem handling them. I must admit that it was most entertaining to see the fur fly!

Next, I was paired with each of the raptors. I'm about the same size as the raptors so our sessions were a bit more even. The raptors are a little stronger than me, but I'm more agile. My longer arms and quicker feet gave me an advantage to elude their strikes and kicks. I did have to wear a protective suit to avoid being bitten by their primary weapon, sharp teeth. I managed to maneuver around back of Rex and get him into a headlock and choke hold. Rex immediately tapped out. With Tara, it was not so easy. She was a bit smaller, but faster than Rex. After some wrestling around, she ended up on top of me with my arm locked behind my back. I gave up. Rex commented, "She does that to me too." Finally, I try and wrestle with Leo. That was a complete failure! Leo just pounced on me, and the match was over. I think that the small cats had the best idea. Run!

During the sessions, Skip was hanging on the ceiling acting as the unofficial referee. If a match got out of hand, Skip would make a loud clicking sound. That was the signal to stop the action and start over. This looked like a good role for Skip, I'm not sure how he would fare wrestling one of us with those skinny legs of his. Later I would find out that Skip had retained an evolutionary self-defense mechanism. He can bite with paralytic venom. That's a pretty good self-defense mechanism. I'm glad that I did not have to deal with that in a sparring match! By the end of the session, we were all exhausted. It was time for another dip in the pool.

Saturn

It's now two, time cycles later and we are preparing the ship for the portal jump to Saturn. From our current position, four hundred and fifty million miles away, Saturn and its rings can clearly be seen without any magnification. I'm on the bridge with Felicia, Leo, Tara and Rex. Felicia asks Tara to lock in the coordinates for a location just above the outer ring of Saturn. Once the coordinates have been determined, they are fed into the portal generator.

Rex is at the portal generator control. He activates the generator, and a circular window begins opening in space, just ahead of the ship. We can see our destination through the portal. Felicia gives the instruction to enter the portal. Leo is at the navigation, making the necessary adjustments to the photon drive. The ship enters the portal and instantly we are orbiting Saturn just above its outer ring. All I can say is, "Wow!" From our pre-jump location, Saturn's rings had a very defined appearance. Now that we are close, they look like a collection of orbiting rocks, ice and dust. Saturn itself, looks like a huge glowing, multicolored striped ball.

I'm thinking about the first time that Galileo, observed Saturn's rings through his telescope. His mind must have been blown. Now I'm in the Starkitty1 orbiting just above the rings. It's an overwhelming experience. I think, *thank you Felicia for bringing me here!*

Felicia says, "Great job everyone, we have arrived at this beautiful planet. Now it's time to start looking at some of the moons."

I'm sitting at the instrument panel that has been receiving readings from a probe that we projected into Saturn's atmosphere. The readings are coming back now. The atmosphere is almost entirely nitrogen and methane. Temperatures near the core are around -300 degrees F. Saturn is not a good candidate for life. One moon does look very promising. That moon is Titan. I already know that the Huygens space probe launched by the European Space Agency had collected a lot of data from Titan. There are rivers and lakes of liquid methane on Titan's surface. There was also evidence of a water ocean thirty miles below the icy crust. The surface is extremely cold and does not contain liquid water. However, it's possible that another form of life could exist in the methane lakes and rivers. Titan's atmosphere is believed to be mostly nitrogen and methane.

After consulting with Leo, Felicia tells us that we will be visiting Titan. In some ways it's like Europa. We found a lot of life in Europa's sub-surface ocean.

Now we will be checking out Titan's sub-surface ocean.

We begin our approach to Titan. The atmosphere is hazy looking, but our instruments can see right through the haze. The surface is rugged looking and there are large dunes in some places. We locate a large methane lake and send a probe to sample its contents and look for any life contained within it. The probe confirms very simple microscopic life forms but nothing substantial. This is not surprising because of the extreme cold and lack of liquid water.

Felicia calls a meeting of the crew to discuss if we should initiate a mission into the sub-surface ocean of Titan. She points out that the concentrations of chemicals in the water could be vastly different from the ocean of Europa. The temperature of the water would likely be different too. This would mean that the life forms that they encounter could also be different. That is if there are any life forms at all. We all agree that a probe should be sent down into the ocean. After the measurements are taken and evaluated, we can decide if a direct exploration is warranted. Leo comments, "Grrr, hopefully our probe will not be eaten this time!"

Titan

Felicia, Milo and I are all riding in the Fastcat2 shuttle. We have just now projected into the sub-surface ocean of Titan. It's a good bit darker in here than in Europa's ocean, so we turn on our lights to illuminate the water around us. The probe that was projected into the ocean ahead of us survived and was able to provide coordinates for the shuttle to safely project in. Milo is at the controls of the shuttle. He gently guides us along. We turn on our infrared vision screen and can now see a good distance in all directions. Like on Europa, there are vents in the ocean floor that expel large amounts of gas and water vapor into the ocean. We also observe several rock formations that connect the ocean floor with the surface crust above. We did not find structures like these in the area that we explored on Europa. The ocean on Titan appears to be shallower than Europa's ocean. Perhaps that explains the difference.

As we approach the formations Milo comments, "I think that those two rising formations ahead of us form the entrance to a massive cavern." The magnified display seems to support Milo's observation. I say, "Why don't we take a look inside?" Felicia says, "Milo, go for it!" Milo begins to guide the Fastcat2 into the cavern entrance. The entrance appears to be about a quarter mile wide. Once inside the cavern, we do not see a far wall. In fact, the cavern width expands outward. There does not appear to be a gas pocket above the water. We continue to navigate into the cavern at a slow speed. Clouds of small, transparent creatures begin to pass in front of the Fastcat2. Under magnification, they are similar in appearance to guppies. The creatures have short bodies, long tails and small mouths. The lack of an eye indicates that they may well be blind. It's possible that as a group, they help each other navigate the cavern using some other means of communication. There are millions of these creatures in each cloud that we pass. I can't wait to see if a next level predator will show itself.

A little deeper into the cavern we finally see a larger creature. It is swimming towards us. Then it stops directly in front of our ship. We slow the Fastcat2 down and bring it to a halt. The creature resembles an octopus, but with ten tentacles instead of eight. It is large, maybe five feet long. The creature is not transparent either. The head contains two very large eyes. It must be able to see us on the other side of the window because it is retaining its position directly in front of us.

I decide to name this creature a decapus owing to its ten tentacles. The decapus is looking intently at us. The eyes have an intelligent air about them. The decapus reaches out with one tentacle and touches the front window of the Fastcat2. Then it slowly pulls the tentacle away. In moments, more of the decapus arrive. They take turns swimming up to the Fastcat2 and touching the window. It's almost feels like they are greeting us. Soon there are about two-dozen decapus congregated in front of the window. Then, almost as if on cue, they all begin moving away from us as a group. At first, we do not follow so they stop moving as if to say, "*Come on slowpoke!*" Milo starts up the drive and we begin slowly moving towards the group. They immediately resume moving forward. I comment, "Gee, I wonder where they are taking us?"

We are moving deeper and deeper into the cavern. Soon more decapus join the group. We have decapus in front of us and on all sides. There must be hundreds of them. Ahead of us, the cavern splits into two sections. The lead decapus group takes a turn to the right and we follow. This segment of the cavern is a bit narrower. It's perhaps five hundred feet wide but then gradually widens again. Soon we begin to see round mounds dotting the sea floor and walls of the cavern. There are openings in the mounds, and I can see decapus swimming into and out of the openings. Felicia says, "I think that they are taking us on a tour of their habitat. A moment later, we find ourselves passing over a very large vent. I look at the instrument panel and note that the water temperature has been rising ever since we entered the decapus habitat. The vent appears to be their heat source. There are also millions of small creatures swarming around the vent.

A group of Decapus is swimming around the vent and appears to be harvesting the creatures.

Felicia comments, "They have built their habitat around the primary sources of warmth and food. I would say that these creatures are quite intelligent. I add, "And friendly too. They do not display any fear of us." Milo says, "Perhaps they have nothing to fear. They are likely the lords of this cavern."

We linger around the cavern for a while and then turn around so that we can head back out. The decapus realize that we are leaving. Some of them rush out ahead of the Fastcat2 as if to say, "*Let us guide you out of the cavern so you don't get lost.*" So, with the decapus in the lead, we navigate back to the entrance of the cavern. They stop and begin swirling around in a series of patterns. This appeared to be their farewell message to us. Milo steers the Fastcat2 back towards the open ocean. Soon after, we opened a portal and are projected into orbit next to theStarkitty1. We dock moments later.

The following cycle, Bella pilots the Fastcat2 back into the cavern. She has the rest of the crew with her. They also receive a friendly reception and tour from the decapus.

Our exploration of Titan proved to be rewarding. We discovered a friendly species of intelligent nautical aliens. No doubt our visit will become a part of their folklore. Perhaps they will even describe us to future generations as benevolent divine beings.

Beyond Saturn

Our next series of stops are on the moons orbiting Uranus and Neptune. First, we enter orbit around Uranus. Leo decides that the moon, Oberon, is a good candidate for a sub-surface ocean. Like other moons we have visited, Oberon is very cold on its surface but also shows evidence of water having erupted and then frozen on the surface. We go into orbit and begin doing scans to confirm if there is a substantial ocean for us to explore. The results come back positive. A probe is projected under the thick crust of the moon. It confirms that there is an ocean located thirty miles below the crust. We prepare the Fastcat2 shuttle for sub-surface exploration.

Tara notifies us that she has spotted a strange feature protruding from the surface of Oberon. It looks like a tube of some sort. We decide to take the Fastcat2 in for a closer look at the tube. Milo, Bella and I are on board Fastcat2. We begin our descent towards the surface. When we are near the protrusion, we begin circling it. Indeed, it is a tube. Under magnification the sides of the tube are covered in dust and ice. The top of the tube is still exposed and appears to be precision cut. It was obviously made by some manufacturing process.

We decide to position the Fastcat2 so that we can look down into the tube. We illuminate the inside of the tube and can see a structure that looks like a door of some sort. It's partially open but there is too little space available to squeeze past it. There is a lot of dust accumulated on top of the door. It's likely that it has been frozen in this state for a very long time. Nevertheless, it indicates that at some time in the past, someone was here and likely had access to the interior ocean of Oberon using this tube. Perhaps it was some sort of lock system.

Our curiosity is up now. I ask Felicia and Leo if we can project into the sub-surface ocean to find out more about who built the tube and lock. They agree. First a probe is sent into the ocean to make sure that it is safe to go in. Felicia and Leo are satisfied that it is safe. We are projected into the ocean. We begin steering the Fastcat2 towards where we would expect to find the other end of the tube. What we find blows our minds. Before us is an enormous dome stretching up from the ocean floor to just below the icy outer crust. We can see the tube emerging from the bottom of the crust and into the dome. There are irregular shaped holes in the side of the dome that appear to have been impacted or blasted away. As we get closer, we enter the dome through one of the holes. We are inside the dome now. Below us are the remnants of a small city that appears to have been abandoned long ago. Many of the structures show signs of damage.

Others are toppled over. It's obvious that a civilization once thrived here. But they either abandoned their city long ago or it was destroyed for some reason. This was the last thing that I expected to see on a moon almost two billion miles from Earth. We spend the next few hours scanning and recording everything we can within the domed city.

This alien city reminds me of the ancient Mayan cities in South America that were suddenly and mysteriously abandoned more than a thousand years ago. Archeologists have been trying to figure out why the cities were abandoned. It could have been disease, war, drought or political upheaval.

After completing our exploration of the alien city, we begin searching for more evidence of the alien presence in this world. We find another domed city. It is a bit smaller and contains an area where the aliens had dug in towards the planet's core. Perhaps this was a mining operation of some kind. Further exploration reveals other smaller domed cities. All appear to have been abandoned long ago. We note that the level of chemical toxins in the water near the cities is quite high. These are levels that would be toxic to most known life forms. Perhaps there was an environmental catastrophe on Oberon that made this world no longer livable. If so, where would the survivors have gone? That is if there were any survivors. There could also have been a conflict that resulted in the poisoning of the aliens and the destruction of their cities.

Later, aboard the Starkitty1, we gather to reflect on the worlds that we had visited so far. Leo points out that each world had spawned life in a submerged sea below the crust even though the surface is totally inhospitable. He says, "Grrr, life finds a way to come into existence and survive. But life is fragile. So, if the delicate balance of the environment is stressed too much, it can be just as easily swept away." I'm thinking about how similar Leo's thinking is to that of the environmentalists back on Earth.

Our final stop in Earth's solar system is Neptune. Neptune is mostly gas and thus unlikely to contain life. This is a similar scenario to the other gas giant planets that we have visited. We turn our attention to Neptune's moons. Leo suggests Triton is a potential harbinger of life, but not on its extremely cold surface. Perhaps below the crust it may be warm enough for some form of life to exist? We do some scans to see if there are any underground bodies of water or other liquids that we can explore. The scans indicate a very low likelihood of finding anything that would be suitable for exploration. Any pockets of water under the crust are too shallow to project into.

Felicia and Leo suggest that perhaps it is time to branch out to one of the nearby star systems. There is a star referred to on Earth as Moss 356. Moss 356 is twenty-five light years away from our present position. There are two planets in the habitable zone. The planets revolve around each other. Felicia points out that no Meowmax spaceship has traveled to Moss 356 yet, however, there have been probes sent there. The probes have been receiving interesting radio transmissions. The two planets in the habitable zone are relatively close to each other. We all agree that we are ready for a new adventure. We will explore the two planets.

Jess

I find all my shipmates fascinating. Each is an alien being with unique characteristics. But of all of my shipmates, the one that intrigues me the most is Jess. Jess is unique. No one else can change shapes and show up at the oddest times. Yet, I feel some sort of connection to Jess, but I just can't put my finger on what it is. Certainly, the story about how Milo found Jess on a comet is just crazy. I mean, what was Jess doing riding on a comet! So, I decide to find out more about Jess.

My first attempts were to ask my shipmates if they had any additional insights about our shape-shifting companion. They all told me the same comet story. Finally, Felicia suggested, "Billy why not ask Jess directly?" So, I took her advice. One day I'm in the exercise room and notice Jess in the corner doing the shape-shifting thing. Rather than just watching, I call over to Jess. "Jess, hello. I was wondering if you wanted to talk?" Jess was presently in the form of a nightstand. A blob rises from the top surface of the nightstand. It forms into a human face. The lips begin to move and Jess replies. "Sure Billy, what do you want to talk about?"

I reply, "For starters, is Milo's comet story true? I mean to say, did he really find you streaking through space on a comet? Did you really slip into the shuttle so that Milo could take you away from the comet? Jess replies, "Yes Billy, the story is true. I'm thankful to be on this ship with kind crewmates like you." I then ask Jess, "How did you find yourself on the comet in the first place? How long were you on the comet? How did you survive? Where did you come from originally?"

Jess pauses before answering. Then Jess says, "Billy, I really do not remember how long I was on the comet. Maybe forever? I can survive in space and everywhere else that I have been since then. I truly do not have any clear recollection of my origin. I do get flashbacks now and then of being in a different place, but none of it makes sense.

Felicia once speculated that I could be a god of some kind because I simply exist. I may even be immortal. But to tell you the truth, the life that I care about really began when Milo found me. When I came aboard, I was immediately accepted as a member of the crew. For that I am grateful."

I'm truly touched by what Jess has been telling me. Then I ask, "How did you acclimate so quickly to life on the Starkitty1? You can communicate with a variety of aliens. You can do the card-dealing thing. While I'm talking to you, I am sensing that you are a very genuine person."

Jess understood that it was important to understand the ship and the crew. So, Jess accessed the computer ship system and absorbed all the information available. Jess learned the culture and history of each crewmember's home planets. Then Jess studied all the ship manuals to understand operation of every onboard system.

Jess says, "Billy, I must go now. Skip and I will be doing routine maintenance on the life support system. Skip likes to have me around to get into those hard to access spaces that he does not fit into. I can also form into a custom tool when needed." I say, "Bye Jess." Jess replies, "Billy, I really enjoyed our conversation. I'm happy that you joined the crew." Jess reverts to blob form and exits the recreation room. I'm left thinking about this wonderful yet mysterious entity. I think, *"Maybe Jess is a God!"*

Moss 356

Felicia is sitting in the captain's chair. Sitting next to her is Leo. I'm stationed at the portal generator control. Tara and Rex are manning the navigation stations. Rex works out coordinates for the jump into the Moss 356 system. The coordinates are fed into the portal generator. On Felicia's command I activate the portal generator and a portal begins to open up in front of the ship. We can see open space, and a star out in the distance. Leo says, "Grrr, that's Moss 356!" Felicia tells Tara, "Proceed." A moment later, we pass through the portal into the Moss 356 system. It's hard to fathom, but we just traveled twenty-five light years in just a matter of seconds.

Felicia asks Tara and Rex to map out our location in the Moss 356 system. The large display above the window is now showing the star, two planets and our ship's position in the system. Leo says, "Grrr, there are two planets in the habitable zone. Let's set a course for the planet nearest to our current location. That is Planet B. Later we can visit Planet A." Felicia says, "Make it so!" Tara gives me the coordinates for the next projection, and I open another portal. I can see Planet B through the portal. It appears to be very Earthlike. There is a large blue colored ocean and a few large landmasses. Felicia says, "Proceed!" Tara guides us through the portal and just above high orbit of Planet B. Leo comments that there are a few satellites orbiting the planet below our position. Felicia tells Rex to reduce our detection profile so that we will appear as space debris if someone on the planet is monitoring objects in orbit.

Felicia tells Tara to put us in high orbit. She calls over to Milo and Bella who are at the science station. She says, "Begin monitoring the planet and determine capabilities. I want to know how advanced their space technologies are. Also please develop a profile regarding the nature of these life forms. We need to know if they are advanced enough that we can contact them directly, or if passive observation is the safer option." Leo comments, "I agree. We need to have a clear picture of life on this planet before venturing any further."

It's an hour later and I'm back in my quarters. I'm ready to begin resting when suddenly, the ship is rocked. Felicia's voice comes over the intercom. "The ship has just been hit by a powerful energy beam. The hull has held, but we need to get out of orbit quickly. Raise the shield." Just as she has finished her announcement, the ship is rocked again, but this time more violently. I'm thrown up towards the ceiling and feel an impact on my head. At first, I feel a sharp pain. The room goes dark, and I feel myself sinking into a dark oblivion. Then I feel nothing, no sensation at all. Then, my life begins to play in my mind. First, I am sitting at the table talking to my parents and sister about my first day of middle school. I tell them that the middle school buildings are larger than elementary school. The kids in the higher grade levels are much bigger than I am.

Following that, I'm standing in the batter's box getting ready to bat against a pitcher from a rival high school. The pitch is thrown directly at me. I try to dive out of the way, but it hits me square in the middle of my back. It really stings.

In an instant, I am in my back yard meeting Felicia for the first time. Then I am in grad school presenting my doctoral thesis to my professors at Stanford. Next, I'm at NASA riding in the high-g force simulator. After that, I'm in the lander headed to the surface of Mars. My life continues to play on. I ask myself, *"Am I alive? Is this what happens when you die? Does your life get played back in your mind?*

Suddenly, the dreaming stops. I have another sensation. It is a feeling of wellbeing. I'm calm now, no cares in the world. I feel that I'm being protected somehow. My mind is in a state of total relaxation. No pain, no worries, nothing but a feeling of warmth. This feeling continues. I see a bright round light. Then the round light undulates as it transforms into the form of a woman. She is glowing. There is a kind smile on her face. I ask her, *"Are you an angel? Am I in heaven?*

Slowly I begin to regain consciousness. Initially my vision is blurry, but then it begins to clear. I'm in my quarters, lying on my bed. I'm looking up into a vision of grace and beauty. The face of a beautiful woman is gazing down at me. I ask, "Who are you? Where am I?" The woman replies, "Billy, you are on the Starkitty1." I ask, "Who are you?" but then I immediately know the answer. Before the woman can answer my question, I ask, "Are you Jess?" The woman replies, "Billy, I am Jess."

My thoughts are racing now, but my mind is so much clearer than it was before I struck my head on the ceiling. Something has changed. I ask, "Jess what happened?" Jess replies, "The ship was attacked. Two powerful energy beams struck the ship without warning. The energy beams originated from what we believe to be orbiting defense satellites. The crew located on the bridge control room got thrown around but were otherwise not seriously injured. Tara immediately took us out of orbit and flew in an evasive pattern until we got out of range of the defense satellites. Felicia asked all crewmembers to report in. everyone reported except you. The computer records showed that you had gone to your quarters just before the first energy beam struck the ship. I came to your room as quickly as possible. I smashed through the door and found you unconscious and bleeding on the floor. I had to act immediately to save your life. Technically, your body had died, but your brain was still active."

I say, "So I was dead." Jess continues, "You were clinically dead. To revive you, I decided to envelop your body inside mine. On Earth, you could describe this as being inside of a protective cocoon. Having done that, I was able to detect all the areas where your body was damaged. I began healing all the injuries that I found." I ask, "So you essentially brought me back from the dead?" Jess replies, "I had never done this before, and I did not know enough about the human body to fix only the damage from the trauma you experienced, so I fixed all your genetic flaws. Wherever I detected a dangerous mutation, I corrected it. Don't ask me how I did it because I have never done a body repair on this scale before. Up until now, I have healed crewmembers of bone fractures, cuts and burns. I think that I have corrected any physical ailments you have now. I corrected diseases that you may develop in the future. I also opened additional memory capacity in your brain by removing a small but growing tumor."

I say, "Jess, why has your appearance changed? You look like a beautiful angel" Jess replies, "When I connected with your mind, I also connected with your emotions. I encountered a vision of female grace, power and beauty that you have kept inside yourself. I hope you are not angry with me for having done that. I wanted to appear pleasing to you when you regained consciousness." I reply, "Jess, I could never be angry with you. You are my guardian angel. Are you going to stay this way?" Jess replies, "Billy, only if you want me to. I can still change into other shapes, but my memory will retain this human form whenever the need arises." I look up at Jess and say, "If you read my deepest thoughts, you probably know that I am lonely inside. For much of my life, I have searched in vain for a soul mate." Jess replies, Billy, I have also been lonely for as long as I can remember. A comet is a lonely place." I look into her eyes and say, "Jess, I'm in love with you." Jess replies, "The feeling is mutual."

Felicia

Felicia calls a meeting of the crew in the break room. Jess is present in her new human form. Felicia is not happy that the Starkitty1 was attacked without provocation or warning. She says, "Billy would have died had Jess had not quickly intervened and saved his life. Good job Jess! More of us could have been seriously injured or killed. I for one do not think that this unprovoked action should be left unpunished. We have every indication that the inhabitants of this planet are technologically advanced and are aware that other space traveling life forms may exist in this galaxy." Leo adds, "I agree with Felicia, at the very least, they could have given a warning to stay away from their planet. Had we received a warning, we would have happily complied. What they did was wrong, and we need to make it clear to them that there are consequences for their actions."

Skip says that there is some damage to the outer hull of the ship. The damage needs to be fixed before the ship can be operated at full capability. The damage was to a sensor array. Felicia says that she and I will put on our space suits and go outside the ship to replace the damaged sensor array. Skip has brought a spare sensor array from the hold. It should be easy to remove the damaged one and replace it. I'm excited because this is the first time that I will be going out into space since the Mars mission. It will also be fun to do a repair job with Felicia. I can't wait to see what she looks like in a spacesuit.

Felicia and I go to the hold. We don our spacesuits. I almost crack up when I see Felicia's furry cat face in the clear visor of the helmet. I pick up the spare sensor array. Felicia has the attachment tool in her paw. Together we walk over to the decompression chamber. Once we are inside the chamber, the door closes behind us. Then the door in front of us opens to the vacuum of space. We are both tethered to the ship in case one of us begins to drift away. We maneuver along the hull of the ship until we arrive at the damaged unit. Felicia uses her tool to loosen up the attachment bolts. Then she removes the damaged array and hands it to me. I hand her the new array, which she attaches to the hull of the ship using her tool. The job takes but a few minutes. Felicia gives me a high-five. Then we pull on our tethers until we are back at the decompression chamber. Once back inside the ship, we remove our space suits. Felicia smiles at me and says, "Great job Billy! I see that NASA taught you well. I reply, "Piece of cake! It was fun doing a repair job with you!"

Now it's time for a little retribution on the defense satellites. This time we will be going in with our shields up and weapons systems locked and loaded. Felicia says, "The planetary defense authorities need to learn to be more hospitable. Let's take out a few satellites and see how they react.

Felicia asks Milo and Bella to present their intelligence report on the inhabitants of the planet. They have been monitoring planet wide communications. These have been fed into the universal translator program. The program is a piece of advanced artificial intelligence software that looks for communications with themes common to other cultures. From there it compares greetings and other commonly found expressions. From these it creates a list of common sounds and words, which it analyzes. The output of the program is a rough translation of what is being said. Over time the program learns and improves on its translations.

Bella begins the report, "The occupants of this planet call themselves the Bromar. The planet is called Bromarus. The Bromar have a humanoid appearance. They stand about five feet tall. They have two legs and two arms. Their feet and hands have six appendages that function similarly to human toes and fingers. The Bromar head is a bit larger than a human head. They have two eyes and flat nostrils on the front of their heads. There is a mouth below their nostrils. Skin pigmentation ranges from blue to green. Milo is at the console and displays a photo of a group of Bowmar on one of the large screens in the control room.

The Bromar developed sub-light space travel capability and have explored and colonized their moon as well as their twin planet Paxon. Paxon appears to be somewhat of a rival now. We discovered what we think are news reports of a space battle between Bromar ships and their enemy. We presume the enemy to be the Paxon. There is evidence of damage to one of the cities on the surface of Bromarus. Felicia comments, "So we may well have strayed into an interplanetary war zone. That explains the defense satellites orbiting Bromarus."

Bella goes on to say that the weapons technology of the Bromar is based on high energy pulsed beams. "As we found out, their weapons are quite effective, however, with our shields activated, we believe that they cannot damage the ship. We recommend always having the shields up when approaching either Bromarus or Paxon."

Leo speaks next. He says, "Grrr, given the hostile setting, we need to present ourselves as friendly. I suggest we first send messages to Bromarus that include images of friendliness. The images should include ones of our crew together in harmony. Milo and Bella can use the universal translator to compose a message of our peaceful intentions. Felicia responds by saying, "I agree, we will approach Bromarus again, transmit the messages and await their response. Tara and Rex will be at the weapons station, ready to respond if we are attacked again, Jess will be at the life support console and Skip will be at the controls for the photon drive. Leo and Billy will man communications and navigation. Let's begin our approach."

The ship is on a heading back towards Bromarus at maximum sub-light speed. The messages and friendly images are being transmitted to the planet. As we near Bromarus, we slow our approach. Thus far, there has been no communications in response to our messages. Then we are once again hit with energy beams from a half dozen defense satellites orbiting the planet. This time the shields are holding up against the attack.

Felicia tells Tara, "Tara, activate the energy pulse cannons. Target the satellites that fired the energy beams at us." We hear half a dozen short high-pitched sounds. This corresponds to the firing of the photon energy cannons. The display screen in the right wall was monitoring the defense satellites that attacked us. In a moment all six satellites explode.

Felicia says, "Do not take any further offensive actions. Let's hold our position in orbit for now. Keep sending the message, let's see how they respond now." I tell Felicia, "I just detected a group of five ships that have departed the surface of the planet. They are headed our way at a fast speed." Leo says, "Grrr, we will soon see if they are still hostile towards us or not." The answer comes soon enough when the lead ship fires an energy beam at us. The impact on the ship is minimal because the shields are dissipating the beam energy. Two other ships fire their energy beams with the same result. Felicia says, "Hold fire for now. Rex, execute a series of evasive maneuvers and short portal jumps. Let's show them that we can easily evade their attacks. The Starkitty1 disappears and then reappears at a location five thousand miles from its last position. It takes a few minutes before the attacking ships figure out where we are and correct their course. They begin firing at us again. Rex executes another portal jump and again, the ships correct course and attack once more.

Felicia says, "Well I guess they are not going to give up so easily." Then she says, "We will have to make them disappear. She says, "Rex, activate a portal in front of the lead ship and the two others that have been firing on us. Project them halfway back towards the planet. Let's see how they react to this demonstration of our portal technology."

In moments, the lead ship and two others vanish. The remaining two ships break off the attack. Our display shows the three ships that we projected away from us have reappeared closer to the planet. They are flying back towards the planet's surface. Felicia says, "Rex, well done! I think that this must have convinced them that it is futile to attack our ship. I suspect that the next communication will carry a more friendly tone."

We remain in orbit for a few more hours. It gives us an opportunity to do more of an assessment of the Bromar satellite technology. We also do some in depth observation of the planet. We detect considerable movement near the surface of the planet. There are ships at sea and planes in the skies. The Bromar are certainly an advanced culture.

I detect a single spaceship exiting the atmosphere. This time the ship is approaching more slowly and is sending a message. The message says, "Intruder, why have you come here? Are you from Paxon? Why have you violated the sacred space around Bromarus?"

Leo tells me to send a message stating that we are not from Paxon. We are explorers from other worlds in the galaxy. Our mission is peaceful. We destroyed the satellites because they tried to destroy our ship. We could have destroyed your attacking ships, but we sent them home instead. We request a meeting. I transmit the message exactly as Leo has stated it.

Felicia says. "Billy, transmit a live feed of our control bridge so that the Bromar can see us." Moments after our transmission, a live image is sent from the Bromar ship. There are six beings either sitting or standing in front of consoles. We assume that this is their command bridge. It looks a lot like ours. One of the Bromar steps forward and begins speaking, "I am Kil, captain of this ship. You have violated the sacred orbit of our planet, Bromaus." Kil takes a moment to study each of us. Then he says, "I see that you are not all the same species. In fact, on my planet, you would be considered lesser life forms. Yet you are piloting a spaceship! How is that possible? Is this a clever illusion that has been conjured up by the Paxon?"

Felicia says, "My name is Felicia. I am the captain of the Starkitty1. As we stated in our earlier message, we are beings from different worlds that have a common interest in exploring the galaxy and discovering life on other worlds. We have traveled twenty-five light years to visit your system. We selected your planet for exploration because it is in the habitable zone of this solar system. Do not be put off by our differences in physical appearance. Each of our home planets underwent differing evolutionary paths." Kil responds, "Differing evolutionary paths? Bah! Nonsense! You are devils!"

Kil continues to stare at us, then he says, "How is it possible to travel between star systems? The distance is too great to travel that far. It would take one of our ships many generations to make such a trip." Leo responds, "We have a technology that allows us to jump long distances instantly." There is silence on the other end. Then Kil says, "I do not believe you. Your appearance here is troubling to me. In fact, everything about you is troubling. We have been taught that the universe was created for the Bromar. Ours is the most advanced life form in existence. Am I to believe that we face a collection of alien life forms with capability far more advanced than ours? Our leaders will not accept this. They will say that it is a trick perpetrated by our enemies on the planet Paxon. That is also my belief. We will not be intimidated by beasts!"

Felicia replies, "Kil, please explain to your leaders that our ship is called the Starkitty1. Our mission is to explore nearby star systems and contact sentient species living on the habitable worlds contained in those systems. On my planet of Meowmax, we believe that the universe is filled with intelligent species inhabiting many worlds. That is why we have ventured here. We want to meet you and learn about you. In exchange, you can learn about us. We are hoping that you are open to interact with us. If you do not want to interact, just tell us. The galaxy is large and there are other worlds for us to explore. If you wish, we will go elsewhere. You would lose an opportunity to learn about us. And us of you."

Kil says, "I will return to Bromarus and confer with our leaders. The decision is up to them." Felicia replies, "We will stay in orbit and await your response. Our one request is to make sure that your defensive satellite systems do not attack us again. If they do, we will destroy all of them." The screen goes blank and the Bromar ship turns back towards the surface of the planet.

After we complete one orbital revolution around the planet, I detect that a Bromar ship is approaching. A closeup of Kil's face appears on the main display. Kil begins speaking, "Captain Felicia, our leaders met to discuss your request. It was decided that you must leave our planet immediately and never come back." Felicia says, "That is unfortunate. May I ask why?" Kil says, "Our world is not ready to accept the idea that there are beings in the universe far more powerful than us. It would go against our core spiritual belief that the universe was created for our benefit and exploitation. The leaders have decided that you and your crew are an instrument of the evil ones described in our sacred ancient scriptures. The evil ones are described as half Bromar and half beast."

Felicia responds, "That is most unfortunate, and I must say, your leaders present an ignorant attitude. But we must honor your request. We will depart as quickly as possible." Felicia tells Tara to cut off all further communications with the Bromar. Felicia lets out a loud hiss. Then she says, "Let's take a look at the sister planet, Paxon. Maybe they would be more agreeable to interact with us." Then she says, "This time we will have our shield up when we get close to high orbit."

I must say that this was the first time that I had ever seen an outburst of anger from Felicia. That was quite a hiss that she let out!

It will be another cycle before we reach high orbit of the planet Paxon. Jess and I are walking down the hallway together towards my quarters. Lately, Jess is spending more of her time in human form. I say, "Jess, I have noticed definite changes in my physical and mental abilities. Both seem to be enhanced. And my memory is so much clearer now. In fact, I even remember life events going all the way back to my birth. How is that possible? What exactly happened when you healed me?"

Jess replies, "Billy, when I healed you, I healed everything about you. As I mentioned earlier, you had numerous degenerative conditions that would have begun affecting your physical and mental health many years into the future. You would call these conditions *aging*. You also were not accessing your full mental capabilities due to some small tumors and imperfections in your brain. Those have all been corrected now." I reply, "Are you telling me that I am no longer aging? That I am now smarter than I was before?"

Jess replies, "Billy, you will age, but it will be at a more natural rate." I ask, "What do you mean by a *natural rate*?" Jess responds, "You now have the maximum longevity possible for a human being. Your lifespan has been enhanced." I'm stunned. I reply, "Do you mean that I will live past one hundred years?" Jess responds, "Perhaps several times that. And you will retain your youth for almost all that time span" I'm blown away. I say, "Wow!"

We reach the door to my quarters and enter it. I tell Jess that I am hungry. Jess does not need to eat food, but she can fake it in a social situation. She asks me if it is ok if she practices changing shapes while I eat. I say, "Sure Jess." I go over to the food replicator and order a burrito, chips and salsa. In a few minutes, the replicator has the food prepared and placed on a dish. I take my food over to the table and sit down. While I'm eating my dinner, Jess is going through a series of physical transformations. Each time she transforms into an object, she asks me how accurate her impression is. I point out any obvious errors. In truth, it's hard to tell the difference between Jess and a real object. While I watch her go through the transformations, I think to myself, "I guess this is what life is like when your girlfriend is an alien!"

Later, Jess and I relax together on the couch. I ask the entertainment system to play some mellow music. I have discovered that Jess is fond of jazz and blues.

She begins to transform into her natural fluid state. Jess envelops my body in much the same way as when she healed me of my life-threatening injury. I slip into a state of total relaxation as we merge. I think to myself, *this must be how shape-shifting entities make love. It's awesome!*

The Planet Paxon

I'm back at my station on the bridge. Jess and I are at the navigation controls. Rex is at weapons and Tara is at the communications console. Milo is manning the portal generator and Bella is conducting scans of the surface of planet Paxon. Bella says, "I'm getting plenty of readings from the planet surface. This planet is smaller than the Bromarus. There is an ocean that makes up about fifty percent of Paxon's surface area versus seventy percent for the Bromarus. There are fewer structures on the main continent. The atmosphere is like that of Bromarus.

The Starkitty1 is approaching high orbit. Only a few satellites are detectable. None are taking aggressive defensive action as did the ones that we encountered above Bromarus. We decide to remain in orbit until we are noticed. After a few hours, Bella detects a ship approaching from the surface of the planet. The ship hails us. The language used in the communication is exactly the same that used by the Bromar, thus it is easily translated. The message says, "Aliens, welcome to Paxon, we received a transmission from our spy on Bromarus. The message described an encounter that the Bromar had with an alien spaceship. We presume that your ship is the one described in the message." Felicia tells Bella to confirm that we are the ship described in the message. Tara sends out a live video feed of our bridge. The response is immediate. The bridge of the Paxon ship is displayed on our large display. It is similar to the one on the Bromar ship. One of the Paxon crew steps forward and begins speaking. "My name is Pick. I'm the captain of this ship. We are all from the planet Paxon. I see that our spy on Bromarus has accurately described the crew of your ship. I'm impressed that aliens from various worlds can work together towards a common goal. The Bromar and us are of the same race, yet our political and spiritual differences have made us mortal enemies. I think that we both could learn a lot from your example."

Felicia introduces herself and describes the mission of the Starkitty1. Then she says, "We would like to visit your planet and do a cultural exchange. Pick replies, "We have been expecting you. You are welcome to send a delegation from your ship to follow us down to Paxon. You can meet our leaders there."

Felicia looks over at Leo. He nods in approval. Then she turns back to the screen and says, "The Starkitty1 will remain in orbit, but we will organize a delegation to come down to the planet. We will reply to you once our away team is organized. Pick responds, "Very good. I will await your response."

Felicia tells Tara to terminate the communications. Then she looks at us and says, "I'm a little nervous

111

about sending a large team to the planet surface until I am sure of the intentions of our hosts. On the surface they seem agreeable, but I do not want to take any chances. I will lead our away team and take Billy and Jess with me. We will take the Fastcat2 shuttle. Leo will assume command of the Starkitty1 in my absence. Hopefully the intentions of the Paxons are honorable. If so, we will rotate visiting teams so that everyone has an opportunity to spend some time on Paxon."

The three of us enter the cargo bay where the Fastcat2 shuttle is stored. Before boarding, Felicia turns to us and says, "There is a risk that the Paxon may be hiding their true intentions when they extended their invitation to us. That is why I asked you, Jess, to come along. The Paxon are not aware of your shape shifting abilities. They will likely consider you to be a human, like Billy. If there is trouble, we will need your special abilities to help us get away. Are you ok with that?" Jess replies, "Felicia, yes. I will do whatever is required." Felicia then says, "The Paxon are also not aware of my telepathic ability. If it's necessary, I will use it to communicate my thoughts to the both of you."

We bord the shuttle and project it to a location just outside of the ship. I activate the shuttle's defense shield as a precautionary measure. I'm really excited about this mission, especially since I'm going to share it with my two favorite aliens. Felicia has introduced me to the wonders of the galaxy. Jess has shown me that anything is possible. She is also my companion. I believe that the three of us are ready for any challenge that we could face on Paxon.

Leo calls over to our shuttle. He informs us that a Paxon ship has departed the surface of the planet and is fast approaching our position. Felicia tells Leo that we are ready for them. A few moments later, Pick sends us a message to follow his ship to the planet's surface. We leave orbit and follow the Paxon ship. As we enter the atmosphere, we begin to get a closeup view of the planet. There are a few scattered cities. The largest cities are on the coast of a large continent. The cities all have ports and airstrips. Then we fly over a city that appears to be partially destroyed. In fact, sections of other cities show damage. Felicia comments, "Looks like there has been some fighting here. This must have something to do with their conflict with the Bromar. We saw similar damage on the surface of Bromar, but not as extensive as here.

As we get closer to the planet surface, I see a mountain ahead of us. There is a large opening at the base of the mountain. Pick sends us a message to follow his ship into the opening. I look over at Felicia. She says, "Go for it."

We fly into the opening. Once inside I can see a large landing strip and a tarmac. The Paxon ship hovers and then sets down on the tarmac. We do the same and set the Fastcat2 beside the Paxon ship. I take a measurement of the air outside the ship. The reading is within the tolerance range for both Felicia and me. For Jess it does not matter, because she can survive in any atmosphere or even open space. Her visible breathing effort is just a simulation to maintain the ruse that she is human.

We open the door to the shuttle and step out onto the tarmac. I close the shuttle door by giving a verbal instruction to the remote control built into my suit. Pick and three others walk up to us. Pick says, "Welcome to Paxon. As you can see, we maintain our spaceport inside of this mountain as a precaution against attack by the Bromar. You may have noticed damage to some of our cities. This is the result of attacks by the Bromar. Thus far they have not been able to penetrate this mountain. We have three similar mountain spaceports at strategic locations around our planet."

Felicia asks, "What is the nature of your conflict with the Bromar? It appears that you are both, the same species. From our previous surveillance of Bromarus, we are aware that Paxon was originally settled long ago by the Bromar." Pick replies, "You are correct. We are the descendants of the original Bromar settlers who colonized this planet. Over time, our objectives and beliefs diverged from those of the

Bromar. We are an open society that accepts differing viewpoints. The Bromar are rigid in their beliefs and their social structure. Eventually these differences caused conflict. The Bromar decided that we must be brought into compliance with their traditional beliefs. When we resisted, they tried to use force to bring us back into the fold. The Bromar sent a fleet to arrest our leaders and force us into compliance. We fought back. We were able to turn back their fleet, but not before taking heavy losses. Many died in defense of our freedom. The Bromar see us as a threat to the control they have over their own planet of Bromarus." He pauses and then says, "Ideas spread quickly." I point out that we did see damage to a city on Bromarus. Felicia asks, "How did that happen?" Pick replies by saying, "We had to defend ourselves, so we struck back at the Bromar."

Pick leads us across the tarmac, down a corridor and into a room with a large conference table with chairs. There are three Paxons sitting at the table. Four more are standing around the room. They have the look of security guards. I can see that they are armed. Each has a variety of weapons attached to their belts. The three Paxons sitting at the table rise to their feet. One of the Paxons begins speaking, "Welcome to Paxon. I am Anona, speaker of the governing council. With me are Broga, the minister of our space defense forces. Also, here is Cara, the minister of civil defense.

Please take a seat." Then she looks at Felicia and says, "The seats have a height adjustment on the side."

Felicia introduces herself as the captain of the Starkitty1. Then she introduces Jess and me as two of her human officers. Felicia sends both of us a telepathic message that she does not like the presence of so many armed guards in the room. She also comments that only military and defense ministers are present. She suspects that we are not going to be briefed about the cultural aspects of life on Paxon. This is going to be a military discussion. I'm very impressed by Felicia's assessment of the situation.

Anona says, "I wish that you were visiting Paxon at a time when we are at peace. Unfortunately, our planet is under constant threat from the Bromar. I understand that your ship was attacked while in orbit around Bromarus." Felicia replies, "You are correct. In fact, we were attacked twice. The first attack by defense satellite was unprovoked. It almost killed Billy. We were forced to leave orbit to repair damage to our ship. When we returned to orbit, we were prepared to defend ourselves. We were attacked once more. We destroyed six defense satellites that had fired on us and were able to repel a squadron of attacking Bromar ships. After a brief communication with the Bromar, we were asked to leave and not return. Apparently, our presence was contradictory to their beliefs. They thought that we were either agents of the Paxon, or demons."

Anona replies, "You see our problem then. We do not hold the same beliefs as the Bromar. They cannot tolerate our dissention. To them, we are heretics that must be punished and brought back into the fold." Cara then says, "The Bromar have sent fleets to punish us and depose our leaders. Thus far, we have been able to repel their invasion attempts." Broga says, "The Bromar have partially destroyed our cities and have forced us to move our space defense ships into caverns like this one. Should the Bromar return, we do not know how long we can hold out. We lost many ships during their last invasion attempt. Our fleet is diminished."

Felicia then asks, "Why have you asked us to meet with you? It does not appear that we are here for a cultural exchange." Anona replies, "Felicia, we are at a great military disadvantage to the Bromar. They have more ships and more advanced weapons. We are fighting for our survival. We need help." She pauses. Then she says, "Your ship has demonstrated vastly superior capabilities to anything that we or the Bromar have. There is a rumor that your ship has the capability to make a whole fleet of ships disappear. With your ship at our side, we can surely repel another invasion attempt by the Bromar. Better yet, we could destroy their fleet and eliminate the Bromar threat to Paxon."

Felicia responds, "Anona, we are explorers, not military. Our ship is equipped with defensive capabilities, and we are governed by rules that we are not to get directly involved in planetary disputes of any kind. We only act in self-defense. We try not to bring harm to anyone."

Anona replies, "Felicia, that is most unfortunate. You have felt firsthand the violence of the Bromar when they attacked your ship. I was hoping that you would be more sympathetic to our cause." Then in a threatening tone, Anona says, "Please reconsider your response."

Felicia says, "Anona, as I said earlier, we cannot do that. We can offer to help as mediators, but we cannot get directly involved in this dispute."

Anona turns to the guards and nods. All at once, they pull out weapons and point them at us. Anona says, "You leave us no choice, you will remain our captives and will not be released until you order your ship to provide us with weapons technology that will allow us to defend ourselves against the Bromar. You must understand that our situation is desperate."

Felicia speaks telepathically to Jess. She asks Jess if she would be able to disarm the guards quickly. Jess replies that she could. Felicia tells Jess to stand by for further instructions.

Felicia says to Anona, "Please tell your guards to put their weapons away." Anona replies, "I cannot do that." Felicia looks at Jess and nods. Suddenly Jess begins to melt into a blob. The Paxons are shocked by what they are seeing. Their eyes have an expression of horror. In seconds, Jess extends out four tentacles that quickly grab the weapons out of the guard's hands and crushes them. The tentacles drop the crushed weapons on the floor. Next the tentacles grab the four of the guards and throws each of them against the walls of the room. Anona, Broga and Cara are all frozen in fear. Felicia says, "Thank you Jess!" Then she looks at Anona. "Anona, you have made a terrible mistake in trying to kidnap us. The first officer of our ship has orders to not deviate from our primary mission. He also can facilitate our escape should we be captured." Felicia then speaks to her communication vest and says, "Leo, now!"

In an instant a portal opens up. Felicia, Jess and I step through it. The Paxons are left wondering how we could just vanish into thin air. We reappear inside the Fastcat2. I fire up the photon drive just as a portal opens in front of the shuttle. I fly the Fastcat2 into the portal. The Fastcat2 disappears from the tarmac and reappears in space near the Starkitty1. A few moments later another portal opens, and we find ourselves transported inside the hold of the ship.

I say, "I love that portal generator." Felicia comments, "Thank Tara and Rex. They mapped out every movement that we took since leaving the ship. When I gave Leo the necessary signal, they put the escape plan into motion. That is how we were able to open so many portal jumps in quick succession."

That leaves me with a question, *what is our next move? Do we leave this system right now? Or do we offer to mediate the dispute between the Bromar and the Paxon?* The answer comes during a meeting later in the day. Felicia begins by recounting the events that occurred on our visit to Paxon. She says, "I'm inclined to just leave this system and let the Bromar and Paxon settle their differences on their own. We certainly do not want to take sides in this conflict. Both sides cannot be trusted." She pauses and then continues, "On the other hand, we could offer to help facilitate a resolution to the conflict if both sides are agreeable. Let's stick around for a few orbits of Paxon and see if we get approached. In the meantime, we will keep the shields up in case someone decides to attack us."

Jess and I are walking down the corridor on the way to my quarters. I tell Jess that I was amazed at how quickly she reacted when Felicia gave her the signal to disarm the guards. "Jess, how did you know what to do in that situation." She replies, "Billy, shuffling and dealing three decks of cards was good practice." I respond, "Really? Dealing cards?" Jess gives me a sly smile. She says, "I had to be fast to be sure that you and Felicia were not harmed."

We enter my quarters and walk over to the couch. We both sit down. Jess puts her arms around me and whispers in my ear, "Let's make love the human way!" I reply, "No complaints from me!" I think to myself, *I must be the luckiest guy in the galaxy!*

On the next orbit around Paxon, we receive a transmission from Anona. She says, "Captain Felicia, we just received a warning from our spy on Bromar. There is a large fleet of ships on the way here. We need your help to avert destruction. Please, do not leave us alone to face them."

Felicia replies, "We will stay in orbit, but will not intervene directly in the conflict. We will act as a facilitator to help diffuse the conflict if both parties agree to participate." Anona replies, "There will be no negotiating with the Bromar. They cannot be trusted. You must join us to destroy them!" Felicia replies, "If you do not want us to facilitate a resolution to the conflict, we will be on our way." Felicia tells Milo to cut communications. Then she says, "Let's stick around and see what happens."

After several orbital cycles, Tara reports that a large fleet is approaching our position. She says that one of the ships has conducted a scan of our ship. As soon as the scan is completed, the fleet begins slowing down. One ship breaks away from the rest of the fleet. It is heading directly towards our position. Felicia puts out a call to all crewmembers to man their duty stations. I run down the hallway and find Skip sleeping on the ceiling. I give Skip a nudge to wake him up. I say, "Skip, sorry to wake you, but we are at battle stations. We will need you to be ready by the photon drive in case we need to increase power." Skip replies, "Sounds serious. I'll get to my station right away!"

When I get to the bridge, I find everyone at their stations. Felicia tells us that she wants to try and encourage the two parties to begin talking instead of shooting at each other. Tara reports that a fleet has just departed from Paxon. Contrary to what we were told by Anona and her ministers, the fleet is the same size and capability as the Bromar fleet. Leo says, "Grrr, there is a lot of lying and deceit by both sides of this conflict. I would not trust anything either party says."

Felicia tells Tara and Rex to try and create a communications link between both fleet leaders and our bridge. It takes some time, but eventually we have a live video feed from the bridge of both ships. Kil is speaking for the Bromar. Broga is speaking for the Paxon. Felicia begins by saying, "You both are on a path towards mutual destruction. We favor neither side in this conflict but instead offer to facilitate negotiations towards a peaceful resolution. Keeping in mind that both parties have been hostile towards us, we will maintain our shields and have weapons at the ready."

Kil says, "We have no desire to negotiate with the heretics of Paxon. They have proven to be a corrupt and godless lot. The only acceptable resolution is subservience or destruction." Broga responds, "That is what I would expect from a race of vile, pious murderers. We will fight you to the last Paxon if necessary!" The insults go on until Felicia says. "Enough! We will remain in our position for one more hour. Then we will depart. You have that amount of time to come to your senses."

Both ships return to their respective fleets. Felicia tells Tara to keep the communications channels open. If there is no answer from either fleet leader in an hour, we are to leave the area at maximum photon drive. The hour passes. Milo is at the photon drive control. Skip reports that the photon drive is ready to operate at maximum efficiency. Felicia tells Milo to accelerate to fifty percent of maximum sub light velocity. Milo says, "Aye captain Felicia." The Starkitty1 is putting distance between itself and the two planets. Meanwhile, Rex has been scanning the sector where the two fleets had been located. He reports that there are multiple energy emissions and explosions. Felicia hisses and then says, "I think that I have had enough of the Moss 356 system. Hopefully our next system will be a bit more harmonious." Then she asks, "Leo, do you have some suggestions for our next exploration?" Leo responds, "Grrr, we have several good options for our next star system to visit. The best one is called Tora 568. It has an Earth sized planet orbiting a yellow dwarf star. The planet is located dead center in the habitable zone." Felicia says, "Good. We can meet up later and review Leo's data on Tora 568. For now, let's take some time off for recreational activity. I feel like a workout and a swim in the pool. Anyone up for a card game later tonight?" Jess says, "I'm ready to deal!"

We all head over to the recreation center for a workout and swim. Jess gains buoyancy in the pool by creating an air pocket inside of her body. I find that to be an imaginative trick. She is a pretty good swimmer too. Of course, she does not need to take any breaths while swimming.

Later, Jess and I are relaxing on the sofa in my quarters and listening to some blues music. I ask Jess, "Have you thought about what you want to do with the rest of your life?" Jess responds, "Billy, I really live in the moment. I existed on the comet for so long that I had no perception of how much time had passed. Then I was rescued by Milo and brought to the Starkitty1. That is when my life truly began. Later, I met you. Everything is new to me. You could call this being born again. I really do not have a concept of what having a future means. One thing I do know is that I enjoy being with you more than anything else that I have experienced." I reply, "So being with me is better than existing on a comet?" She replies, "I see, that was meant to be a joke. Correct?" I say, "Yes, it is. Your learning!" Jess replies, "Ha! Ha!" I say, "I'm glad that you like being with me" I give Jess a hug. Soon we both drift off to sleep. At least I do. I'm not sure if Jess sleeps because whenever I wake up, she is already awake and practicing her shape shifting.

I have been showing Jess three-dimensional holographic images of common Earth objects. She can shape shift into those shapes with ever increasing attention to detail. Once she has a shape done correctly, it is easily replicated in a few seconds. This ability is very much like muscle memory. She never forgets how to do it again.

Tora 568

The Starkitty1 has projected into the Tora 568 star system. Leo reports that there is a planet in the habitable zone that has many characteristics for sustaining life. The planet has water, a favorable atmosphere and climate suitable for supporting life. Tora 568 is about thirty light years from Earth.

Skip and Jess have been doing some routine maintenance on the photon drive. A few parts are beginning to decrease in efficiency, so they need to be replaced before we continue any further. The parts requiring replacement are in a tricky location. Jess uses her shape changing ability to transform into a thin fluid form and squeeze into a small conduit that leads to where the faulty parts are located. She removes the faulty parts and replaces them. Then she oozes back out of the conduit. Skip is happy with her work. Otherwise, a lot of disassembly work would have to have been done to access the faulty parts.

The next morning when I wake up, I see Jess in the middle of the room practicing her shape shifting transitions. She hears me rustling around, so she transforms to her female human form. I walk over and give her a big hug. Then I grab some food from the replicator. Moments later, Leo's voice comes over the intercom. It's time to man our stations for the jump to the habitable planet orbiting Tora 568. Jess and I step out into the hallway just in time to see Skip walk by on the ceiling. He says, "Good morning, Billy and Jess. Back to work!"

We head down the hallway to the bridge. Tara and Rex are right behind us. Felicia, Milo and Bella are already at their stations. Leo says, "Grrr, everyone gets situated, "We are about to make the jump to a planet we suspect may harbor life of some kind. There is water present on the surface. There is also an atmosphere like the one on this ship, and the temperature is warm, but still tolerable for life to thrive." Tara says, "I have coordinates that will place us in high orbit around the planet." Rex replies, "The projector is locked onto the coordinates." Leo says, "Grrr, make the jump!"

Immediately the image in our main view screen changes from a background of millions of stars to a view of an earthlike planet. Leo says, "Grrr, Milo, begin scanning for radio signals. Bella, scan the surface of the planet for signs of life." Moments later, Milo says, "I'm getting some radio transmissions from the planet. So far, the universal translator has not been able to decipher them. Leo says, "Grrr, let's hear them." Milo says, "Here goes."

The sounds that we hear are a series of scratching and clicking sounds. I comment, "That sure sounds a lot like one of Skip's symphonies." Felicia says, "Skip, what do you think of these sounds? Can you speculate as to their origin?" Skip replies, "I have been listening in. The source must be from an insect or arachnid type of species. I must say that it's quite melodic. Whoever created it has good taste." I give Leo a funny look. He rolls all six of his eyes. Then Leo says, "Grrr, Milo, try and compare the sound to the various music tracts that Skip has stored in the entertainment system. I believe that we have translations of the lyrics from some of the songs. This could help the universal translator to come up with a translation. This approach works. Soon we get a translation.

The translation begins, "Greetings to the orbiting alien spaceship! Welcome to our planet, Entorus. We call ourselves Entorans. Please confirm that you have received and understood this message." Felicia tells Tara to send a confirmation message stating that we received the message. The confirmation also describes the Starkitty1's mission of peaceful exploration. It is accompanied by a video of the crew interacting with each other. The video includes Skip walking around on the ceiling." Moments later there is a response, "My name is Clack. I am the chief science minister for Entorus. We are fascinated by the diversity of your crew. You are of several different species. One among you appears to be an arachnid." Our legends tell of a great arachnid who travels throughout the heavens and will someday walk among us on Entorus."

Tara responds, "The arachnid you speak of is named Skip. Skip is the chief engineer on our ship. Skip would like to address you using his native language." Skip begins making a series of clicks and scratching noises. The translation appears on the monitor. Skip is greeting the Entorans in a language that is filled with poetry and musical tones. Skip's vocals are accompanied by a series of physical movements. It is basically a spider song and dance routine. The Clack responds, "Skip, you express yourself so eloquently! We would be honored to have you and your crewmates visit us on Entorus. We will send a ship to meet and escort you to our spaceport."

Sometime later, The Fastcat1 and Fastcat2 are projected into orbit near our ship. An Entoran ship rendezvous with us and begins escorting our shuttles to the planet's surface. Milo is piloting the Fastcat1 with Jess and I aboard. Bella is piloting the larger Fastcat2 with Skip and Felicia aboard. For now, Leo, Tara and Rex remain on the Starkitty1.

There is cloud cover over the portion of the planet that we are approaching. As we descend through the clouds, a city composed of thousands of large mounds appears below us. Each mound has widows, and doors. The largest mounds are concentrated in one area of the city. The city is located on the coast of a large continent. There is a harbor with hundreds of boats docked. Mountains ring the city on three sides. I can see major transportation arteries that are full of vehicles. The city reminds me a bit of Los Angeles, but with large mounds where large buildings would be. As we get closer, I determine that many of the roads are mass transit lines. When they approach the center of the city, they appear to underground tunnels.

Just ahead of us is a spaceport featuring a large tarmac. Sitting on the tarmac are hundreds of spaceships and air ships of varying sizes. This is our destination. We follow Clack's ship to the tarmac, hover briefly, and then land. I perform some atmospheric tests to confirm that the air outside the ship is safe to breath. I tell Felicia, "All clear to depart the ship." Felicia says, "Skip, the Entorans seem quite taken with you. I think that you should lead our group when we talk to the Entorans. Do you agree? Skip replies, "Yes, captain. I can do that."

The door to our shuttle opens and we step out onto the Tarmac. Clack approaches followed by a large group of Entorans. The Entorans are very similar in physiology to Skip with the exception that they are a little bit smaller in stature. We all have our universal translators dialed into the Entoran language. Clack says, "Welcome to Entorus, we are honored to have you all as guests on our planet. Our leaders are anxious to meet you all, especially Skip." Skip replies, "The pleasure is ours." Clack beckons us to follow him.

One of the first things that I notice is an apparent lack of security. The Entorans are by all appearances, an insect species. I do not see any evidence of weapons or military regimentation. Entorus appears to be a peaceful planet. There are numerous Entorans scurrying about on the tarmac. We approach a large mound that has an opening at ground level. A crowd of Entorans congregates around us. Their attention is mainly focused on Skip. As we pass, they emit a clicking noise that sounds like applause. I say to Felicia, "I think that Skip is a rock star here!" She responds by asking, "Billy, what is a rock star?" I pause for a moment and explain, "On Earth we sometimes call popular individuals rock stars." She replies, "Oh, that's very good."

We are guided into a long wide corridor. Entorans are walking all over the place. Some are on the ceilings and walls. For now, Skip walks on the floor with us. We turn into a large chamber. Here we are greeted by a small group of Entorans. They must have been waiting for us. One Entoran introduces herself as Fana. She tells us that she is the current elected leader of Entorus. Fana introduces us to Bert, the director of this city. Fana and Bert each extend a leg. Skip does the same. I say to Felicia and Jess, "This must be an arachnid handshake." I am impressed by how easily Skip is fitting in with the Entorans. It's as if he is coming home. Perhaps Skip, or his ancestors originated from Entorus or a related planet.

Bert offers us a tour of the city. We are led back out to the tarmac where we board a type of hovercraft. It has viewing windows all around and underneath it. The craft is powered by rotating jets. The pilot powers up the jets causing the craft to rise into the air. Soon we are flying low over the city. Bert points out various points of interest. There are prominent buildings, a kind of open-air stadium, parks and other recreational facilities. Bert tells us that even more of the city is underground. We can take the subway system later to visit those areas. We are given a brief history lesson on how the city was built up gradually over time. Skip is really excited by all that he sees here. He is finally among his own species. Skip is fascinated by how the Entorans live and work.

When the underground tour begins, we board a vehicle resembling a tourist bus. The transportation tunnels are all have good lighting. We see underground buildings that rise from the floor of the tunnel to the ceiling above. We are told that there are dozens of levels below the surface of the planet. Large structures begin at the lowest level and pass up through many levels to the planet's surface. This city is a three-dimensional labyrinth, yet the Entorans seem to get around without getting lost. As we reach the outskirts of the city, we come upon ancient ruins.

Bert tells us that it is believed that thousands of years ago, the planet was populated by a humanoid type species. A calamity befell their civilization. It was an extinction event of some type because all that is left of the civilization is the remnants of ruined structures. Bert says that there are low levels of radiation in certain locations in the ruined city. Later, the arachnids quickly evolved to become the dominant species on the planet. They built their own cities on top of and next to the ruins of the humanoid city.

As I look at the ruins, I think about how much they resemble a human city that might have been bombed or set fire to. Then I think about the warring planets in the Moss 356 system. Is this to be their fate too?

After the tour is over, Skip tells Felicia that he would like to stay on the planet for a few more days. She agrees to his request. We are all sensing the strong connection between Skip and the Entorans. Felicia, Jess, Bella, Milo and I return to the shuttles. Bert agrees to show the rest of our crewmates around the city tomorrow.

The following morning, Milo pilots the Fastcat2 back to the planet with Leo, Tara and Rex aboard. Skip is there to greet them when they land. With Skip are Clack, Fana and Bert. Over the next few days, we make additional trips down to the surface. We are treated to a sporting event in the stadium. It is a game that looks like a cross between soccer and rugby. There is a ball, which the Entorans kick around with their legs. There are goals of various sizes on each end of the field. The game has no timeouts. When a goal is made, the ball is immediately put back into play in a random location on the field. When the time limit expires, the game is over.

We attend an opera which is a bit excruciating to listen to because of all the loud scratching and clicking sounds. Of course, we act as gracious guests. Leo comments to the Entorans, "Grrr, the music and lyrics were excellent! Such talent!"

The last day before we are to leave, Skip asks to speak privately with Felicia. He begins by saying, "Felicia, the time that I have spent here on Entorus has been the most satisfying of my life. I feel totally accepted here. I also believe that I can contribute to their technological development. In turn, they have treated me like family." Then he says, "I provided a DNA sample to their genetic science lab. The result came back yesterday. My DNA is a very close match to that of the Entorans. We are of the same species with just minor differences. I want to stay here on Entorus." Felicia responds, "Skip, I was suspecting that you might want to stay here. You certainly have my blessing. I must say that I will miss you, as will all your shipmates. But we will all be happy that you found a place where you can establish you roots."

After we say goodbye to Skip and the Entorans, the Starkitty1 breaks out of our orbit and back out into open space. We are traveling at sub light speed using our photon drive. This has been a very satisfying visit. Meanwhile, Leo is still working out the next star system for us to visit.

The Anomaly

I am on the bridge manning the long-distance scanner. Everything has been going normally today. Our next destination has not yet been determined so we are cruising along in space at sub-light speed.

Suddenly I detect an anomaly out ahead of the ship. I'm getting a power reading that is greater than anything that we have encountered in our previous travels. The anomaly is located about fifty thousand miles from the ship. It just suddenly appeared out of nowhere. I report the reading to everyone on the bridge. Felicia asks Tara to get a visual on the anomaly. Tara replies, "I just got a lock on the anomaly. It's on the large display screen now." We look at the display and see a pulsing, round black phenomena of some kind. Felicia says, "Magnify." The image becomes larger as we zoom in." I report that the power readings are fluctuating wildly. Felicia asks, "Anyone have an idea what that might be?" Leo says, "Grrr, I have done a lot of space exploration, but have never seen anything quite like this. It looks like a large portal, but much more dynamic in its behavior. Portals do not put out such massive energy readings. They do not pulsate either." Tara and Rex also confirm never having seen such an anomaly. A search of the computer memory also provides no explanation of what this anomaly could be.

I report that the anomaly has begun moving towards us very quickly. Felicia says, "Let's put some distance between ourselves and the anomaly. Make it a jump of one million miles." Rex is at the portal controls. He opens a portal, and we instantly jump one million miles away from our previous position. So, we moved one million miles, but the anomaly is exactly in the same position relative to us as it was before we made the jump. We are all shocked by this development. I report, "The anomaly is still gaining on us."

Felicia orders a further jump of five million miles. I again report that the anomaly still is gaining on us. The anomaly jumps exactly when we jump. It's doing this without the benefit of a portal generator. The anomaly is now five thousand miles away. Felicia says, "It appears that we cannot outrun the anomaly so we might as well sit here and find out what it is." Then she says, "Shields at maximum!"

I report that the anomaly continues to move towards us. Then, it comes to a stop just in front of the ship. The anomaly continues to pulse and give off wild energy readings. The anomaly is completely black, and we cannot see anything inside of it.

Our predicament is that the Starkitty1 is sitting in space with a huge pulsing black anomaly in front of it.

We cannot escape from the anomaly, and we have no idea what it is or why it has pursued us.

Then Felicia receives a telepathic message. It says, "*Come in my child.*" Felicia tells Tara to maintain our distance from the anomaly. Several minutes pass. Then, the message is repeated. "*Come in my child.*" Suddenly, The Starkitty1 is pulled inside the anomaly. The background of stars has vanished. We are suspended in a black nothingness. Leo says, "Grrr, Tara, make sure to track every movement that we make inside this anomaly. It may be the only way to find our way out." Tara says "Leo, no worries, I began tracking our movements as soon as the anomaly pulled us in."

Felicia asks, "Any suggestions on what to do next?" Leo suggests that we focus on collecting as much data as we can from the anomaly." I report that the energy readings have suddenly gone to zero." Tara says, "I have tracked our movement while inside the anomaly, but I have no idea where we are within the galaxy. I cannot locate any known star or planet. It's as if we were thrown into an alternate universe that is empty of anything except ourselves and our ship." Felicia responds, "Maybe the anomaly is a door into an alternate universe!" The thought is quite scary. Leo comments, "Grrr, we cannot use the portal generator to escape because we have no idea how to determine our current position in space, let alone any destination coordinates."

Felicia says, "Just before we were pulled into the anomaly, I received a strange telepathic communication. It said, *'Come in my child.'* Then I received it again a few minutes later. Is it possible that the anomaly that swallowed us up is a living, conscious entity of some kind? If so, maybe we can communicate with it." Then she says, "Tara, open a communication channel. Adjust the transmission power to maximum. Send a message out on all communications wavelengths. Include translations to all known languages." Tara responds, "What do you want the transmission to say?" Felicia replies, "We are peaceful explorers, please talk to us!"

Then Felicia addresses us. She says, "Our mission is one of exploration. We strive to visit distant star systems and encounter other life forms that inhabit those star systems. It is possible that the anomaly that swallowed the Starkitty1 is in fact, a life form. If this is so, we must learn more about it. That is why we are attempting to contact it. Hopefully this can be done without jeopardizing the lives of everyone on this ship." Felicia's talk helps us to focus on the job at hand.

We remain in our current position inside the anomaly while the transmissions are being made. Time passes, but we have not yet received a response.

Felicia asks everyone to be patient. Rex is at the communications station when a return transmission is detected. He notifies Felicia and the rest of the bridge crew. Jess and I are relaxing in my quarters when we hear Felicia's voice on the ship's communication system tell us to come to the bridge immediately.

In moments, all of us are assembled on the bridge. The displays are showing views of space outside the ship. All we can see is emptiness. I report that I'm measuring power fluctuations again. These seem to rise and fall in synch with the transmissions that the ship is receiving. Felicia asks Rex if he can get a translation of the transmissions. Rex replies, "I am running them through the universal translator. I'm getting an output from it now. I will play the audio." A scratchy voice can be heard. It says, "Welcome three-dimensional beings. To facilitate your understanding of me, I will ask you to call me Zax. You no doubt are confused by the emptiness that surrounds your ship. Your three-dimensional perception is limiting what you can perceive. Allow me to adjust my appearance so that you can better understand what I am.

In a moment, the total blackness of the space around us is transformed into a dimly lighted space containing untold numbers of black portals. There are also billions of small flashes of bright light swirling around the ship and then streaking off into the distance. Zax explains, "What you see are portals linking to millions of locations in three-dimensional space. The flashes of light are entities composed of entirely of psychic energy.

If you pass through any one of the portals, you will arrive in a location many light years from where you journey began. I have observed that you have a portal generator on your ship. Your portal generator can open a single portal consisting of an origin and a destination in three-dimensional space." Zax pauses and then continues. "I have observed your ship during each portal jump." Felicia replies, "Zax, are you telling me that when we do a portal jump, we are actually traveling through a kind of multi-dimensional space?" Zax replies, "You are correct. But because the portal that you generate has one fixed origin and one destination, you pass in and out of multi-dimensional space instantaneously. At least, that is how you perceive the transition. But because time does not really exist in multi-dimensional space, I can easily perceive your movements during each of your jumps. This has allowed me to learn more about you." Leo asks, Grrr, what is the purpose of so many portals?" Zax replies, "I observe the universe through the portals. I can even use the portals to transmit messages intended to be received by certain individual entities."

By now, my mind is totally blown away. Am I really hearing this? Is there more to the universe that what our limited minds can perceive? Is the passage of time just an illusion? Then I think, "*Is Zax God? Is this multi-dimensional space really heaven? Are the flashes of light individual soles?*"

Felicia asks Zax, "Why did you pursue us and then freeze us here in multi-dimensional space? Why did you call to me telepathically to *come in my child*?

Zax replies, "Like you, I am curious about all that exists three-dimensional space. I wanted to meet the beings that have so frequently moved through the portals. I also was impressed at how such a diverse group of alien species can live in harmony and care so much about each other. So many other advanced species have fallen into conflict and subsequently perished. I decided to bring you here for further examination." Leo asks, "Grrr, so, you are as curious about us as we are about you?" Zax replies, "Yes. That is correct. The challenge for me was to determine how to capture and then communicate with you in this multi-dimensional space. Initially, I tried to communicate telepathically. Felicia replies, "That was when I received the message, *come in my child*." Zax continues by saying, "That is correct." But you did not immediately enter the portal that I created. So, I tried once more to communicate and then decided to pull you in. Later, when you began your transmissions, I was able to decipher their meaning. That is when I responded, and we began this discourse."

Leo says, "Grrr, Zax, it's very nice to meet you, but at some point, we are going to want to return to the point in three-dimensional space where we were before you pulled us in." Zax replies, "You have been able to track your ships movements while inside multi-dimensional space. You can leave by jumping to the earliest point where you began tracking. The exit portal will be there in front of you.

Then Zax says, "Felicia, before you leave, I hope that I can learn more about how your scientists on Meowmax developed and then perfected portal technology." Felicia says, "The information you seek is contained in our ships' computer memory. I can transmit the pertinent information to you. Would that satisfy your curiosity?" Zax replies, "That is acceptable." Then Zax asks, "Could you also transmit some of your history? While I have observed many worlds using the portals, there are gaps in my knowledge. Also, time does not behave the same here as it does in three-dimensional space. In fact, time does not really pass at all."

Leo says, "Grrr, Milo, please check the ship's chronometers. Has there been a passage of time measured since we entered the anomaly?" Milo checks all the ships' chronometers and replies, "Leo, the chronometer has stopped. It appears to be frozen at the precise moment that we left three-dimensional space. Jess then says, "It appears that since we entered the portal, I cannot change shape either. Time must be a critical parameter for shape shifting."

As we monitor the instruments on board the ship, all appear to be functioning, but any time-based measurements are frozen at the exact reading when we entered the anomaly.

After the requested information is transmitted, we bid farewell to Zax and navigate to our point of entry. Before us is the pulsing portal. We exit through the portal back into familiar three-dimensional space. Upon our exit, the portal closes behind us. It is as if it never existed in the first place. The chronometers and instruments begin functioning again. Jess regains her shape-shifting ability. Felicia tells us that just before the portal closed, she received a telepathic message from Zax. It said, *"My children, thank you! I have enjoyed meeting you. Felicia, if you ever need my help, you can open a portal and contact me."*

Later, I am in the recreation room working out on the elliptical machine. Jess is trying out a stationary cycle. I find this quite interesting because Jess really gains no fitness benefit from exercise because her physiology is totally different from anyone else on the ship. She tells me that by going through the motions of exercising she feels closer to me. It becomes an activity that we can share together. Sometimes I get the feeling that Jess wishes she could be one hundred percent human.

Felicia walks into the recreation room accompanied by Milo and Bella. They are so cute together. They each select an exercise wheel. Soon all five of us are working out. I tell Felicia that I thought Zax had many godlike attributes. Felicia says, "The thought occurred to me as well." Then she says, "I wonder what brought you to that conclusion?" I reply that Zax can control millions of portals. In Zax's multi-dimensional realm, time does not appear to exist. I say, "This means that Zax likely has always existed. In contrast, time exists in our three-dimensional world. So, we have a beginning and an end. Lastly, I thought about all those billions of lights swirling around in Zax's realm. Zax described them as *entities composed entirely of psychic energy.* Could those be the souls of living beings who have passed away? Did we visit a kind of heaven?"

Felicia replies, "Billy, I guess that it is possible. Many cultures have depictions of a god who interacts with certain individuals. There are also depictions of heaven. It is also possible that Zax is simply another life form that is beyond our understanding." I say, "Felicia, you may be right about that. Anyway, I'm glad to have had the experience of meeting Zax." I then ask Felicia, "What is our next stop? Felicia says, "Leo has a habitable planet picked out for us. We will jump to it in the next time cycle, so make sure you get a good rest tonight." I reply, "I will do that. Thank you, Felicia."

The next few solar systems that we explore each contain at least one planet in the habitable zone. The habitable planets contained life forms, but none that have advanced to the level of having created a civilization let alone space travel. We cataloged each planet, and the life forms we found there.

We were approaching the end of our mission of exploration. Felicia is anxious to get back to Meowmax before she enters her fertilization cycle. Bella also is about to enter hers. I ask Felicia if she and Bella have mates back on Meowmax. She replies, "We share Milo. He is a perfect mate. He is very intelligent as well as adventurous and brave. We will create very smart kittens!" I reply, "I should have figured that out already."

Leo says that he is looking forward to returning to Meowmax. He will stay there for a while to visit his pride. Then he will look for another exploration mission. They may even give him a ship of his own to command. He says, "Every time that I travel through a portal, I will wave to Zax!"

I ask Tara and Rex what their plans are. Tara replies, "I think that Rex and I are ready to return to our home planet of Trexia. Felicia is letting us take a lot of video and data with us. We will share these with the Trexian space authority. I'm sure that they will be very interested in seeing what we have." Rex says, "Maybe we can get a speaking tour out of this. Or a documentary." I respond, "I'm sure that you two will become famous."

I'm ready to return home to Earth. It's been an exciting journey. And I have spent time with the greatest shipmates that a space traveler can ever have. There is just one more shipmate that I need to talk to about plans for the future. That is Jess.

Jess and I are sitting on the couch in my quarters. I ask Jess, "Have you thought about what you want to do when the mission ends?" She replies, "Billy, I know that you want to return to Earth. Well, I want to go with you. That is if you want me to." I respond, "Absolutely! I want you to come with me to Earth. I can't even think about what life would be without you."

Jess then says, "What do you want to do when we are on Earth?" I reply, "To be honest, I really haven't given it much thought. I just know that I want to spend time with you. Earth will take some getting used to though. There aren't any shape shifters on Earth. You will have to be careful about doing transformations when humans are watching. Earth is not like the Starkitty1." Jess says, "I think that I can manage."

Then Jess tells me that she has been having more of the flashbacks lately. Her life prior to being on the comet is slowly coming back to her. I tell Jess that maybe I can help her regain her memory. I suggest that she envelope me so that our minds merge together. Perhaps then I can help her open those lost memories.

Jess is hesitant at first. She tells me that she is a bit afraid about what she may find out about herself. Perhaps she had done something evil in her past. I assure her that I do not think that she would be capable of evil. Finally, she tells me that she is ready.

We go over to my bed. I lie down and Jess begins to transform into her liquid form. She flows over my body. Soon both of our minds join. It is a very powerful experience because I can feel her emotions and thoughts and she can feel mine. I can read her thoughts as though they are mine. I also clearly visualize what Jess sees. The images of her memories are so vivid and precise. It's as though they are happening to me.

Suddenly, my senses are activated. I am on the comet moving quickly through space. It is rocky and cold. I can see stars all around me. Off in the distance, a spaceship approaches. It's the Starkitty1. A shuttle is launched. I recognize it as the Fastcat1. The shuttle approaches and lands nearby me. The door opens and an individual wearing a white spacesuit walks out. I feel an urgent need to draw attention to myself, so I begin to do a series of shape transformations. The individual notices and walks towards me. I can see through the transparent shield on his helmet. I recognize the furry face and bright eyes of Milo. Milo spends some time observing me. Then Milo walks back towards the shuttle. I feel an overwhelming desire to follow him. As soon as Milo opens the door, I move past him and enter inside the shuttle. This memory begins to fade.

Now another memory enters my mind. I'm not on the comet. Instead, I'm in a laboratory. Several blue humanoid type aliens in white lab coats are moving around me. I feel my body undulating as I initiate a transformation. There are instruments arrayed around me and probes attached to the surface of my body. The aliens have hand-held devices. They are entering instructions into the devices. Each time, I feel a stimulation to move another part of my body. I have a sense that I am very young. I'm not entirely sure of what is happening to me. I feel like I'm part of an experiment. Or maybe, I am the experiment!

Another memory enters my mind. I'm in another lab. The blue aliens have set up a target at the other end of the room. The target is in the shape of an alien. The target alien has an appearance that is different than the aliens in the room. It is thinner and has a reddish skin color. Its facial features are also different from the blue aliens in the white lab coats. I am given a verbal command from one of the blue aliens. I immediately extend a tentacle arm, lash out and slash the target into pieces. I hear chattering from the blue aliens. I sense that they have approved of my response. This memory also begins to fade.

I'm in the same lab now. The blue aliens are dragging out a live red alien. The alien is trying desperately to shake loose from their grip. They shackle the red alien to the wall on the far side of the lab. The red alien is clearly distressed. One of the blue aliens in a white lab coat gives me a verbal command. I understand that I am to extend a tentacle and slash the red alien apart. I experience a feeling of pity for the red alien. This red alien is not an inanimate target. It is a living being. I just stand there and refuse to obey the blue alien's instructions. The blue alien appears to be angry. Once more it yells the verbal command to attack the red alien. Again, I refuse. The blue alien presses a button on his hand-held device. I feel a sharp pain. I understand that I am being punished for my non-compliance. After receiving several more painful stimulations, I am angry. I lash out at the blue alien. I destroy his hand-held device and throw him hard against the wall. Other blue aliens attack me. I grab them and throw them around the lab. Suddenly I feel a great shock. A powerful beam weapon has struck me, and I am paralyzed. When I recover my senses, I'm inside a dark confined space. Is this some kind of prison cell or cage?

After a long period of confinement, the cage I am in opens. Outside the opening there is a rocky desolate terrain. I flow out of the cage and onto the rocky terrain surface. All around me are stars. I am alone now. No blue aliens, no lab, no red aliens. I am exiled to this comet, doomed to travel through space for an eternity.

I'm lying on the bed now with Jess next to me. She has separated from me and changed back into human form. The experience has been exhausting. Jess speaks to me. She says, "I now understand how I came into existence. The blue aliens in the white coats created me. I was an experiment, an artificial intelligence prototype. They were trying to create a living, shape-shifting weapon that they could control and use against their enemy. But I refused to comply with their commands. I rebelled, so they exiled me to the comet as my punishment. There I stayed until Milo rescued me." I say, "Jess, you see now that even back in the first days of your creation, you had a sense of right and wrong. You refused to kill an innocent red alien that had done you no harm. Instead, you lashed out at the evil ones. The price you paid was a long, terrible loneliness on the comet, but you were rescued and brought into the light." Jess replies, "And my reward was finding my shipmates and you. Thank you for helping me to unlock my past, painful as it was." I say, "I'm here for you Jess. You are very special."

Parting

The Starkitty1 is in orbit around Earth, I realize that my journey with Felicia and my crewmates has come to an end. I have experienced so much since departing Earth two years ago. I will never forget Felicia and the crew. On the other hand, I do miss Earth. There are so many things that I want to do here now that I have space travel out of my system, at least for now. But what will I say to people when I return? I don't think that I can just start talking about where I have been the last two years of my life. People will think that I'm crazy.

I do have one idea. There is a way to tell my story and not get sent to the funny farm. I can become a science fiction writer! I will create fictional characters, but the stories that I tell will be accurate. I decide that I will use my real name as the author instead of creating a pen name. That would certainly draw readers to my stories. I was somewhat famous (or infamous) before I left Earth to join Felicia on a romp around the galaxy.

I am a bit concerned about my finances though. When I left Earth, I had just a small amount of money to my name. I have a checking account at a local bank, and I put the rest of my money in a double tax-free municipal bond mutual fund just before I left. I gave instructions to let the interest be reinvested. This way my tax liability would be minimal for the time that I am gone.

Jess and I are relaxing in my room when there is a ring at the door. I say, "Come in." It's Felicia. She steps into the room and begins telling us how much she is going to miss Jess and me. Then she says, "Billy, I will still keep in touch with you by email."

I'm not sure how Felicia manages the email trick when she will be four light years away on Meowmax. It probably has something to do with the probe that she placed near Jupiter's outer ring and a portal generator. I tell her that I will want her to send video of the kittens when they are born. She says, "Absolutely. You and Jess will be at the top of my contact list. Then she says, "I know that on Earth, money is important for survival. That's not the case for us felines from Meowmax. Anyway, we would like to give you and Jess a going away present that will ensure that you will be comfortable when you settle back into life on Earth."

Felicia goes on to tell us that while the ship's been in orbit, she asked Leo to gain access to the Earth Internet. Leo began mining crypto currency using an isolated instance of the ship's computer system. She says, "Billy, we will give you the key to the Bitcoin that we mined for you. There are six hundred Bitcoin in the account that we set up for you. Consider it compensation for the time you and Jess spent as productive members of the crew." I respond, "Felicia, thank you. But you really did not have to do that for us. The time I spent on the ship with you and the rest of the crew was reward enough."

I do accept the gift. I recalled that Bitcoin was valued at approximately one thousand dollars per coin when I left Earth. Upon my return to the planet, I'm shocked that the value now is around thirty-eight thousand dollars per coin. That's over twenty-two million dollars! I'm sure that's enough to get a new start on life!

Just before departure, the crew gathers to say their goodbyes to me and Jess. It's bittersweet. I really love them all. So now I'm ready to portal back to Earth with Jess at my side. Felicia asks, "Billy, do you have a destination in mind? I respond, "How about the bench at Shoreline Park in Mountain View? She replies, "You got it." Tara finds the coordinates and opens a portal. I can see the bench on the other side of the portal. I turn around one last time and wave good-by to my friends. Then I hold Jess's hand and we step through the portal and back onto the Earth. We go over to the bench and sit down. It's late morning and we have some time to relax. Jess says, "So this is Earth? Seems like a nice place." Just then, a flock of geese fly overhead and out to the nearby ponds.

Our first stop will be to walk to downtown Mountain View and withdraw some cash from my bank account. We need to pay for a place to stay for the next few nights. Next, I will buy a computer and work on cashing in some of that Bitcoin that Felicia gave us. The book writing will begin after we have a permanent roof over our heads.

Three Years Later

I'm sitting at my desk getting ready to publish the fifth book in my science fiction adventure series. It's titled, **Space Stories, Volume 5**. I'm surprised at the popularity of my books. Some of the critics love the alien characters. They say that I can bring them to life. Little do they know that the aliens I describe are real! Each of my books made it up to the top of the bestseller list for science fiction.

Jess has shown interest in my book writing. She has added some of her own perspectives to each of the stories. Jess is also my proofreader. Somehow, she has become well versed in writing styles. Jess has read many of the great works of literature, including science fiction works written by Arthur C Clarke, Robert Heinlein, Ray Bradbury and others. When Jess reads a book, she has it committed to memory. She can quote a line in any book that she has read. For example, if I ask her a question about a character in a book that she has read, she will answer the question and recite related passages. Jess also keeps track of the financial side of our book business. She is a great accountant and has the tax code for small business memorized.

Jess is amazing. I'm really impressed at how easily She has adapted to life on Earth. From the moment she made the decision to join me on Earth, Jess began studying all the Earth related information stored in the ship's computer. It did not take long for her to become familiar with the nuances of human culture and human behavior.

My phone rings. Usually, I just listen to the message and do not pick up. It's almost always a scam or a telemarketer. I'm listening to the message this time. The caller says, "Hello, this is Dr. Samar Gupta calling for Dr. Billy Wilson. I am an avid reader of your science fiction novels. I think that they are some of the best that I have ever read. I have a proposition that I'm certain you will find of interest. I would like to fly out and visit with you at your earliest convenience."

I find it interesting that the caller has identified me by my formal title. After all, I do have a doctorate in astrophysics. At this point, I'm really interested in hearing what this fellow has to say. I pick up the phone and say, "Hello, Dr. Gupta, this is Billy Wilson. Please tell me more about yourself and your proposal." He responds, "Billy, I'm pleased to be talking with you. You can call me Sam. I work for a special research division of the government. I'm working on a top-secret project. I have researched your background and read your books. I believe that I have an opportunity that will be of interest to a person with your unique knowledge and qualifications. I would like to fly out to California and give you my presentation in person." I respond, "Sam, I'm a writer so my time is open. Can you fly out here later in the week?" Sam replies, "How about Wednesday afternoon?" I reply, "Deal!"

Before meeting with Sam, I do a search on his name. Sam has a doctorate from Stanford in astrophysics. He is a highly regarded scientist who has worked at many of the advanced R&D labs around the country. More recently, he has also served as a director for a few large labs. I'm really impressed with Sam's credentials. I'm also very interested in finding out why such a high-power government scientist is so interested in me.

Wednesday afternoon I get a call from Sam. His helicopter has just landed at Moffett Field. His driver will be bringing him to my house soon. Twenty minutes later I hear my doorbell ring. I open the door and greet Sam. He is a rather distinguishing looking fellow who appears to be in his mid-forties. Sam is wearing a suit. I'm in a tee shirt and shorts. This is my typical attire when writing. We shake hands and I invite Sam to sit down on one of the comfy chairs in my living room. I ask Sam if he would like something to drink. He responds that a glass of water would be fine. I walk into the kitchen to get two glasses of water. Then I return and sit down.

Sam begins by saying that he has studied all the transcripts and reports from the Mars mission. This includes the many post flight interviews that I was subjected to. Sam says that he has also read all my books. Sam pauses and looks me straight in the eyes. He says, "Billy, after absorbing all this material, I can come to only one conclusion. Everything that you said in the Mars mission interview transcripts is the truth. Furthermore, everything that you wrote about in your books are also true". Sam continues by saying, "I believe that Felicia is a real alien. I believe that Felicia left you a message on Mars. By that, I mean, the message that got you in hot water with NASA. I also believe that the stories you have authored are personal accounts of your actual experiences traveling in space on board Felicia's starship."

I'm floored by what Sam has just said. After a minute of silence, I say, "Sam, what makes you think that the stories are true?" Sam replies, "I have access to satellite data going back decades. On the day that you say you first met Felicia, there was a mysterious observation recorded from one of the orbiting satellites. At first this was thought to be a meteorite landing somewhere in Portola Valley, California. I believe that it was an actual spaceship landing. Some of the other occurrences in the transcripts from the investigations also hold up with satellite data recorded at the time. Your friend Felicia really got around our planet. She was hitting all the top cat related tourist destinations!"

Sam continues, "You disappeared for two years and then suddenly resurfaced. There were no credit card records, no bank withdrawals and no activity of any kind that would indicate that you even existed during that time period. Then, suddenly, you reappear. You file late tax returns, withdraw money and start your life up again. I think that you were traveling in space to the places described in your books. Billy, you are a genuine galactic space traveler!"

Again, I am speechless. Finally, I say, "Assuming that what you say is true, what do you want with me?" Sam says, "What I'm about to tell you is top secret. Only a handful of people in this country know about this." Sam pauses and takes a sip of his water. Then he says, "Billy, I work in a top-secret research facility in the Nevada desert. It is popularly known as Area 51. I'm the director for the research projects that are being conducted there. I'm looking for a pilot with special skills and knowledge that no one else on planet Earth has. But before I can give you specifics of the assignment, I want you to come out to Area 51 and see our facility and the research that we are doing."

This has been a lot to absorb in the short period of time that I have been talking to Sam. Finally, I say, "Sam, your proposal is very interesting to me. I would like to come out and visit Area 51. There is one catch though, I must bring someone along with me." Sam is surprised at my request. He asks, "Who do you want to bring with you? And why?"

I say, "It's a good thing that you are sitting down right now." I look towards a table in the corner of the room. I say, "Jess, its ok to show yourself." The table begins to melt into an undulating blob. Then the blob begins to take on a human form. I can see Sam's eyes widening. In moments there is a beautiful woman standing in front of them. Sam is speechless. I say, "Sam, I would like you to meet Jess. Jess is a shape shifter. We met on board the Starkittty1. She joined me when I returned to Earth." I pause, "Jess and I are in a relationship. Where I go, Jess goes too." I add, "By the way, Jess is an excellent mechanic and a pretty good pilot."

After a short pause, Jess says, "Sam, nice to meet you. I'd love to come and see Area 51." Sam finally says, "Ok, you can both visit. I will be sending a helicopter to Moffett Field on Friday. Billy, I will send you credentials beforehand. But how do I explain Jess to our security team. I'm sure that she does not exist in any of our databases. It would take a bit more time to come up with a new identity for Jess. I reply, "No worries, Jess can transform into a suitcase. I will carry her on board the helicopter. When we arrive inside Area 51, she will transition back to a human form."

Sam replies, "A suitcase?" Billy looks towards Jess. She smiles and then begins a transformation. In moments, a large suitcase, complete with rollers and locking mechanism is sitting where Jess had been standing. I say, "Genuine American Tourister!" Sam looks at me and says, "Ok, sounds like a plan. Jess transforms back to her human form and says, "I'm looking forward to visiting Area 51."

I walk Sam towards the door. We shake hands and Sam walks out onto the front porch. Then he turns around and asks, "Is Felicia really a cat?" I look at him and nod. Then I say, "Meow!"

Area 51

The helicopter puts down at the Area 51 helipad. Sam is parked nearby in a government issued Lincoln sedan. I step out of the helicopter carrying a satchel and a large suitcase. I roll the suitcase across the helipad to Sam's car. Sam greets me and shakes my hand. He opens the rear door and I place the suitcase in the back seat. Sam drives off towards the building complex. On the way, I ask if it is all clear for Jess to make her transition. Sam replies, "Yes, it's ok. The windows are darkened, so no one will be able to see in the back seat. In a moment, Jess is sitting where the suitcase once was. She says, "Hi Sam. I enjoyed the helicopter ride."

Sam turns around and hands both Billy and Jess a security badge and credentials. Then he parks the car in the small parking lot next to his office building. He turns to Jess and says, "You are now Jessica Turner, a newly hired research scientist consultant. She looks at the badge and sees her face on it. He says, "I took the picture when we met at Billy's house. I think it came out pretty good."

Sam asks if we would like a drink or something to eat before starting the tour. I say that I could use a drink and maybe a sandwich. Jess looks at Sam and says, "I don't eat or drink, but I can fake it if the situation requires me to keep up appearances." Sam calls over to the kitchen to bring some sandwiches and a liter of mineral water to his office. In twenty minutes, a man shows up with a couple of paper bags containing the food requested. I begin eating my sandwich. Then I take a bite out of the one designated for Jess. I say, "For appearances."

While I am eating, Sam begins talking. Jess is listening intently. It's funny, but I have noticed that males are a bit distracted by Jess. Her human form is athletic and attractive, but she has an intense air about her when she is focused. People tend to feel challenged by her.

Sam says that a year ago, an alien spaceship landed in the desert near the Area 51 base. The ship was intact and was carrying a crew of three aliens. The ship was spotted as soon as it landed. A team from the base drove out to the landing site to investigate. They set up a large camouflage tent to hide the spaceship. They also began communicating with the aliens. A linguistics expert worked with them to establish a basic language translation. A week later, the ship and the three aliens were quietly brought to the Area 51 base and a special habitat was set up in a large basement laboratory. An artificial environment was set up inside the habitat so that the three aliens could survive there. A gowning room and air lock were built so that humans could dress in special suits equipped with an air supply. The suits were like those used in space, on the moon and on Mars. Then he says, "Initially, the three aliens claimed to be on a mission of peaceful exploration in our solar system. They said that their ship's interstellar drive malfunctioned, and they only had their slower backup drive functioning. They picked Earth as a place to land because it appeared habitable.

Jess asks, "So what happened to the three aliens?" Sam replies, "They seemed comfortable for the first six months. They agreed to transfer some of their technology to us in exchange for the life support that we were providing." I ask, "So what happened after the six months?" Sam replies, "They began to get sick. Two of them died rather quickly. The third alien was near death when he said that he had something to confess. I was called to the habitat where we were keeping him. He admitted that the three of them were not explorers. Rather, they were an advanced scouting ship. They were scouting our solar system when the interstellar drive mishap occurred. Earth was the nearest planet, so they landed here."

Jess asks, "Did the alien explain why they were sent to scout the solar system?" Sam looks at each of us and then says, "They call themselves the Cormac. Their planet is sending an invasion fleet. Earth is the prime target. They believe that with some modification, the Earth is habitable for the Cormac. They plan to exterminate all humans and then alter the atmosphere so that the Cormac can breathe it without wearing any special equipment." I say, "Wow! Did the alien specify a timeline for the invasion?" Sam replies, "All he said was that the fleet is on the way and the invasion will happen soon!"

I ask, "Sam, do you believe what the alien told you?" He replies, "I have no choice but to believe him." He explains that after having received kindness from us, the last surviving alien felt guilty about his role in our impending demise. His confession was done to clear his conscience."

Jess asks, "Sam, where do Billy and I fit into this?" Sam says, "We have the alien ship in a basement holding area. The ship appears to be operational, except for the interstellar drive and a few less important systems. I need someone to fly it. Better yet, if someone can fix the interstellar drive and operate the onboard systems, we may be able to use the ship to detect the invasion fleet and hopefully defend the planet."

I say, "It just so happens that Jess is an expert spaceship mechanic. She was trained on spaceship maintenance by a spider named Skip. Skip was the chief engineer of the Starkitty1. If anyone can troubleshoot an alien spaceship system, it's Jess." Sam replies, "Well, that's a real bonus. Let's get over to the lab so that I can show you the alien ship."

We enter a large concrete bunker style building. There is a single story above ground. Sam leads us to an elevator. He places his hand on a pad and then enters a security code. The elevator opens. We enter and take the elevator down five floors. The elevator door opens, and Sam leads us down a corridor. On the right are large double doors. Sam again enters his security credentials. The doors open to a large chamber. The ceiling of the chamber extends upwards by about fifty or sixty feet. The building appears to have a retractable roof.

Right in front of us is an alien spaceship. At first glance, it looks intact. There is a hatch on the rear of the ship that is open to the floor of the chamber. The ship is large and looks almost like the USS Defiant from the Star Trek DS9 TV series. It has a bridge in the front of the ship that features a large transparent window. The ship has a flat shape. On either side are engines that likely provide propulsion. There are structures on the front, sides and rear of the ship that may serve as housings for some type of sensors or weapons. Several of Sam's engineers are working on the ship. Sam says, "Here is the alien spaceship. My engineers have been working to activate the ship's critical systems. For the most part everything is working except the interstellar drive and the most powerful photon energy weapons. With the help of the last surviving alien, we were able to download the technical manuals and translate them to something that we can understand. The weapons and propulsion technology is way beyond anything that we have ever worked on before so the work is going very slow."

Jess responds, "I have experience working on the photon drive for the Starkitty1. I'll bet that the technology is not too different. I just need to absorb the information in the manuals. Then give me a wrench and I will get to work!" Sam says, "That sounds like a plan. He calls over to one of the engineers and says, "Hey Danny, come over here. I want to introduce you to two people who will be helping us to get this ship operational." Danny walks over and immediately recognizes me. He says, "I know who you are. You are Dr. Billy Wilson the astronaut and science fiction writer. I'm a big fan!" The he looks at Jess and says, "I'll bet you are the shape shifting alien from the books! I always believed that the stories were true. They were so detailed and consistent." I have just one question though. Is Felicia really a cat?" At hearing that, we all break out laughing. Finally, I reply, "Yes, Felicia is a cat."

Danny says, "I can't wait to work with both of you. Together, we will get this bird flying!" Jess says, "I'm looking forward to working with you and your team

Danny." I can see that Danny is starry eyed. Jess has that effect on people.

Danny gives Jess and I a tour of the outside of the spaceship. He points out each feature and its function. He makes sure to tell us which features are functional and which ones they have not been able to get working yet. Jess eagerly absorbs each bit of information that Danny provides. I can visualize how she is cataloging each bit of information and storing it away for future use. Of course, I know little about Jess's physiology so I'm not sure how or where she stores the information. Jess is a truly unique life form.

Next, Danny takes us up inside the spaceship. We begin on the bridge. Apparently, the aliens were quite humanoid in appearance except for their large heads and four digits on their hands and toes. They also were a little shorter than humans. The bridge is therefore easily adapted to human ergonomics.

Danny points out that the aliens breathed air that was composed oxygen and nitrogen, but also a substantial amount of carbon monoxide and other toxic gasses. He says, "We believe that we can adapt the life support systems to only process oxygen and nitrogen in amounts suitable for humans to breathe. " Jess says, "No worries about me, because I don't need to breath. The breathing you see me doing is faked. I don't have lungs. I can even survive in the vacuum of space, so no space suit required." Danny replies, "Noted. That's one less passenger to have to provide life support to." I add, "She's pretty good in a fight too!" Danny responds, "I'll bet she is!"

We move on to the photon drive controls. Jess studies the control panel and then says, "Can I take a look at the actual photon drives themselves?" Danny says, "Sure." We walk down corridor and through a door into a small room. There is a grating on the wall. Jess is staring at it. Danny says, "That leads to the actual photon drive. We tried to crawl in there, but it's very narrow and we would not know what we were looking at anyway." Jess says, "Let me give it a try." Then she says, "Remember that I can transform out of human form into any object or shape that is required to do a job." Having said that, Jess removes the grating. Then her body begins to liquefy. Danny's eyes get real big. Jess flows into the conduit in a liquid form. In a moment, she disappears. Danny just looks at me with big eyes. I reply by saying, "If you recall, this was all in the books." Danny just nods. About ten minutes later, Jess's liquid body begins to flow out of the conduit and onto the floor. In a moment, the liquid rises and transforms back into a human Jess. In her hand is a metallic part.

Jess holds the part out and says, "I think that this is the part that malfunctioned. We just need to replicate it." I say, "Jess, how do we do that?" She replies, "I'll bet that this ship has a 3D printer somewhere that can make us a new one. Let's look at the maintenance manuals."

Sure enough, after reviewing the translated manuals, Jess locates the 3D printer that was built into the ship. It's built into a corner of the storage hold. The roof has several nozzles protruding downwards from it. Below it is a platform. Danny says, "We were wondering what that contraption was for." Jess says, "This is a similar setup as the one on the Starkitty1. When a part breaks, the 3D printer builds a new one from the design files stored in the ship's computer memory. If we can power up the 3D printer and gain access to the computer, we can fabricate our part."

Over the next few days, Jess absorbs all of maintenance information contained in the ship's computer. We activate the 3D printer and fabricate the needed part. Jess then liquefies and performs the part replacement. Meanwhile, I'm training on how to operate the ship's flight controls. There is a virtual flight simulator program in computer memory. By the end of the week, Jess and I are ready to take the alien craft out for a spin.

Sam joins us in the chamber. He wants to watch as we take the ship out on its first flight. I'm at the flight control, Danny is at communications and Jess is at the propulsion controls. Sam goes over to the building's control panel that will open the ceiling door. As the door slides open, we can see the stars above us. I say, "Here goes." I activate the hovering jests and the ship begins to rise up and out of the roof of the building. I'm amazed at how silent the jets are. When we are about one hundred feet off the ground, I say to Jess, "Let's start moving forward, but not too fast." The ship begins to move out over the base and then over the desert. Jess increases the forward velocity. I begin steering the ship through a series of steep climbs and dives. The response is incredibly fast. I love this spaceship!

We are over open desert now, so we accelerate the ship to ten times supersonic speed. The ship does everything we ask it to do. Somehow, our bodies are decoupled from the detrimental effects of fast acceleration. We should be seeing G forces that would make Danny and I pass out, but instead, it's like we are not moving at all. This ship is not quite as capable as the Starkitty1, but it still is impressive. After a few more maneuvers, we return to Area 51 and hover over the building. Then we descend inside. When the ship has touched down, Sam closes the building's roof cover.

We debark the spaceship and I say to Sam, "That was awesome! I think we can fly this ship into space. If we are going to use the ship to defend the Earth from invasion, we are going to need all the weapons operational." Sam replies, "Lets hold that until tomorrow. We can do some target practice in the desert." Jess says, "We really need to give our ship a name." Sam says, "Any suggestions?" Danny suggests, "Why not **Defender**. After all, that is likely what we will be using it for. Defending the Earth."

Sam asks, "Anyone have an objection?" No one makes another suggestion so he says, "Defender is what we will call the ship." Then Sam says, "I'm going on the next flight. I really want a ride in a spaceship. It's my boyhood dream ever since I started watching Star Trek episodes." I reply, "I don't see why not. After all, you're the boss!"

The following morning Jess and I walk over to cafeteria. Sam is already sitting at a table with Danny. They are both having breakfast. Jess and I join them. Sam is wearing a Star Trek t-shirt with a picture of the original Enterprise printed on the front. He looks at us and says, "Beam me up Scotty!" We all have a good laugh.

After breakfast, we walk over to the building where the Defender is kept. After taking the elevator down five floors, we walk over to the Defender. Sam puts his hand on the hull of the ship. He says, "I'm finally going to fulfill my dream to travel out into space."

All of us enter the Defender and get seated. Danny and I go through a pre-flight checklist. Jess reports that she has run the star drive diagnostics, and everything looks good for our flight. Sam has the roof retraction controls loaded onto a hand-held remote. He retracts the roof. In moments, our ship rises vertically out of the building. I begin maneuvering the Defender forward and fly it out over the desert. I tell everyone that I'm ready to take the Defender up into space. In moments, we are headed up at a steep angle. We exit the atmosphere and are soon into the darkness of space. Below us we can see the Earth in all its glory. It's a beautiful blue and white ball suspended in space. I say, "Let's see how fast we can take this ship to the moon. We continue to accelerate until we are traveling at one percent of the speed of light speed. With each passing second, the moon is growing larger and larger. This is much faster than any Earth spaceship or capsule has ever traveled, but it is well within the capabilities of the Defender. It only takes a few minutes to reach our destination.

As we approach the moon, we decelerate and go into orbit. I say, "While we are here, why don't we do some target practice with the energy beam weapons? Any objections?" Sam replies, "We are in space, so no permits or authorization are required. I say, go for it!" We drop out of orbit and swoop down towards the surface of the moon. We spend the next hour picking out targets on the surface and blasting them with photon energy beams. Danny tells Jess, "You did a great job getting the photon energy cannons operational. Look at the size of those craters created by the impacts!" I add, "She did a great job at repairing the interstellar propulsion too. I'm not getting even close to the maximum speed that this ship can travel at."

Sam has been having the time of his life riding in the Defender. He keeps giggling and whooping every time we do a maneuver or fire off an energy beam. Finally, we decide it's time to return to Area 51. We reenter the atmosphere and fly down over the Nevada desert. When we reach the base, we hover over the concrete building. Sam retracts the roof with his remote and the Defender descends inside. When we exit the ship, Sam says, "That was really fun." I say, "I think that we will need a few more flights to get completely comfortable with the capabilities of the ship."

That evening, Jess and I are relaxing on the couch in the apartment that we were assigned. Jess says to me, "Billy, it's nice that we have a spaceship, but it's only one ship. We have no idea how many ships we may be confronted by if the Cormac attack. We also have never flown this ship in an actual battle. We would have the element of surprise because the Cormac fleet will not expect to be confronted by the

Defender. But that will likely not be enough to stop them from attacking the Earth."

I look at Jess and say, "We will need some help if it comes to a confrontation with a large Cormac fleet." Jess replies, "Where will we get help?" I respond, "I will ask Felicia for her assistance. I will send Felicia a message. The message will be directed at the monitoring probe that is in Jupiter's outer ring. The probe uses portal technology to instantly pass messages to Meowmax. Hopefully, it will arrive in sufficient time so that Felicia can contact a special friend who should be able to help us deal with the Cormac fleet." Jess says, "Until then, we will have to prepare as best we can."

Two days later I receive an email response from Felicia. It says, "*Billy and Jess, no worries, I opened a portal and contacted our friend. Our friend has agreed to intervene and diffuse the situation with the Cormac fleet. By the way, we are all doing well here on Meowmax. The kittens have almost reached maturity and are doing well in their elementary studies. I will send photos real soon.*

Love, Your friend, Felicia."

One Billion Miles from Earth

Admiral Heymark is standing on the bridge of his flagship. He is the commander of the Cormac invasion fleet destined for the planet Earth. His fleet is made up of two hundred and fifty warships. They are prepared to attack the Earth and exterminate all the human inhabitants. Once the extermination phase is accomplished, the next phase will begin. The Cormac will alter the composition of gasses in the atmosphere so that it is safe for the Cormac, to breath without having to wear special respiratory equipment. When that phase of the operation is completed, the planet will be ready for occupation by Cormac settlers and miners. The bountiful resources of planet Earth and surrounding planets will be theirs for exploitation.

The Cormac have been observing the Earth for almost one hundred years using scout ships. Recently, one of the scout ships had an engine malfunction and landed on the planet's surface. A distress signal was received but then the signal faded. Admiral Heymark has assumed that the ship and its crew of three must have been destroyed in a crash. Prior to its demise, the ship reported that the Earth did not have any effective space defense systems. That was welcome news. Admiral Heymark is expecting little, if any resistance from the humans. His fleet is presently less than a month away from Earth.

An officer manning the navigation station reports that a large anomaly has just appeared in front of the fleet. It materialized out of nowhere. The anomaly is large, black in appearance and pulsating. The anomaly is emitting enormous amounts of energy. The magnitude of the emissions is greater than what the ships instruments are capable of measuring.

Admiral Heymark asks his bridge crew, "Any suggestions as to what this anomaly is? Does it present a danger to the fleet?" The science officer replies, "Sir, I did a search. There is nothing in our ship's memory banks that describes an anomaly with these characteristics. I recommend that we avoid getting any closer." The navigation officer suggests, "Let's change course and try and navigate around the anomaly." Admiral Heymark says, "Make it so, but first, notify the other ships to follow our lead." The fleet makes a sudden course change. And then another, but the anomaly adjusts its position to counter every course change the fleet makes. The anomaly's course corrections are instantaneous.

Admiral Heymark is concerned at this development. He orders the fleet to fan out. He hopes that this maneuver will allow most of the ships to maneuver around the anomaly. The navigation officer reports that the anomaly is still positioned in front of the ship. The other ships in the fleet begin reporting back that the anomaly is still positioned in front of their ships too.

Admiral Heymark is getting frustrated. He thinks, *how is this possible? Every ship is viewing the anomaly in their path regardless of the maneuvers they make. Is there one anomaly or two hundred and fifty?* Admiral Heymark is pondering the next evasive maneuver when he suddenly senses a telepathic presence inside his head. He is instantly gripped by fear. He thinks, *what is happening inside my head?* Then a voice reaches out to him. The voice says,

"Go home! Now!"

Afterward

It's a Monday morning and I just got out of bed. I am dressing so that I can go over and get some breakfast at the cafeteria. I check emails on my computer. There is one from Felicia. The email contains numerous attachments. I tell Jess to come over. Then I begin reading the message to her.

"Billy, I hope that you and Jess are doing well. Our friend, Zax contacted me telepathically. Zax assured me that Earth is now safe from any threat posed by the Cormac fleet. Zax ordered the Cormac fleet admiral to go home. The leader ignored his order, so Zax projected the entire Cormac fleet to a location fifty light years away. It will be several generations before the fleet will be able to get anywhere close to Earth or their home planet of Cormac.

I attached some photos of the kittens playing with Milo, Bella and myself. They are so cute!

I heard from Leo. He has his own command now.

Milo and Bella send their love.

Keep in touch.

Love, your friend Felicia."

50 Light Years From Earth

The navigation officer reports on the position of the status of the Cormac fleet. He says, "Sir, I have received communications from all two hundred and forty-nine ships. They are all intact. No damage has been reported to any of them after passing through the anomaly. Also, the anomaly is no longer detected."

Admiral Heymark responds, well that is good news. Can we resume our course towards the target system and planet Earth?" The officer responds, "Sir, we are in an uncharted sector of the galaxy. None of the star readings make any sense. I cannot locate our home system or the target system." Admiral Heymark angrily responds. "Well find out where we are then!" The officer responds, "Aye sir, we have the ship computer looking through all the known star charts to get a lock on our position. Based on the analysis, we could be anywhere in a fifty to one hundred light year radius from our last known position before the anomaly swallowed us up." Admiral Heymark responds, "Are you saying that we are lost in space?" The officer replies,

"Yes!"

Dear Reader, if you enjoyed Galaxy Cat, please write a review and/or leave a rating.

You may also enjoy the action-packed sequel to Galaxy Cat: Galactic Liaisons

Thanks,

Barwell Hollings

Made in the USA
Middletown, DE
03 December 2022

16801863R00102